MANCHESTER VICE

JACK D MCLEAN

For Sheila (you know why) and Jeremy (so do you)

I have become a stone-cold killer, or something very much like one.

It beggars belief that only a year ago I was a mild-mannered family man. An ordinary man in an ordinary job, with nothing more sensational to do during the average week than read the Sunday newspapers.

How did I turn into the monster I hardly recognise?

My journey, if you could call it that, began last year on February seventh.

The day I met Jim Kennedy.

I met him in my role as a volunteer prison visitor.

Prison visitors are people who befriend prisoners in the hope that this will help to steer them back onto the straight and narrow. The hope is almost always forlorn, as most criminals re-offend, often within days of getting out.

When I sat down opposite Jim in the Visitors' Centre at Strangeways, he barely acknowledged me. He was dark and sullen looking. Between us was a small grey table, and all around us criminals and family members mingled together.

I introduced myself with a practised cheeriness.

"Hello Jim," I said, "I'm Bradley Sharpe. You can call me Brad."

He looked at me with sadness in his dull eyes. He had good reason to be sad. He was dying of cancer and had been given only months to live. He'd been hoping to be released on compassionate grounds before the year was up, and to spend the last days of his life on the outside, but this had been refused. I'd agreed to provide him with the support he needed to remain positive, or at least something short of suicidal, during the short period he had left.

"Hello," he replied. "Pleased to meet you, Brad."

He didn't look particularly pleased, but at least he was trying.

I wondered how to begin our conversation. I'd thought of a number of opening gambits to get him talking, but I didn't end up needing any of them. We'd both been briefed about each other before the meeting, and this had evidently put an idea into Jim's mind.

"I suppose you know I'm dying," he told me.

"Yes, I've been informed."

"I've been giving it a lot of thought." He leaned closer to me. "I have secrets, Brad, profound secrets that will change the course of history. There's no point in keeping them to myself any more. I've been told I'm not getting out of here. My time is nearly up and I want the world to know all about me. I'd like you to handle my story. You're a newspaperman. You've got the skills to get it published."

I took out the pen and notepad I always carried and poised the pen theatrically over the pad. It seemed unlikely that Jim would have a story worth telling, far less one that would change the course of history, but I decided I ought to humour him to make him feel better about himself.

"What are these secrets of yours, Jim?" I asked. "The sooner you tell me, the sooner I can get to work on your story."

He looked right and left. When he'd satisfied himself that no-one was close enough to overhear, he said:

"You don't have to waste your time writing anything. I've done it all for you. It's in my journal."

"Where's your journal?"

"It's in my house."

I tried not to appear sceptical; I'm not sure I succeeded.

"Won't the police have taken it?"

A sly smile formed at the corners of his mouth.

"They don't know about my house," he replied.

Far-fetched as this statement was, I nevertheless found myself wondering if it could be true.

"You better give me the address."

He hesitated.

"There's something else," he said. "I want you to promise me that you won't publish anything about me until I'm dead."

This was a condition to which I could readily agree. Jim probably had nothing useful to give me in journalistic terms, and if he did, well, I wouldn't have long to wait until he was gone.

"Agreed."

His response was brief and to the point.

"Give me your pen and a piece of paper."

I handed him my black ballpoint pen and a page torn from my notebook. This was strictly against the rules, but no-one seemed to notice, or if they did, they didn't give a monkey's. Jim wrote what looked like a number of Chinese characters on the notepaper and returned it to me with the pen.

"Go to Chinatown, to a Medicine Store called *Chu's Herbs*," he said, "and ask to speak to the owner. Tell him that Jim sent you and show him what I've written. Chu will give you a set of keys to the house. The address is the Old Chapel, Palatine Road."

At my age, pushing sixty, I no longer had the confidence to rely on my memory, so I noted that down.

"This may be the last time you see me," said Jim. "My mission is nearly over. I don't think I'm going to last much longer."

When I left Jim, I headed straight for Chinatown.

As I pushed open the door to Chu's Herbs, a bell tinkled. His shop, I discovered, was little more than a long ill-lit room with a counter to one side. A couple of customers chatted in low voices and a Chinese man wearing a grey suit and a scowl stood behind the counter.

"I'd like to speak to the owner," I said to him.

He looked me up and down.

"I'm Chu, the owner. What do you want?"

I felt faintly ridiculous at the prospect of doing what I was about to do, but I thought that, having come this far, I might as well get on with it, so I furtively showed him the sheet of paper with the Chinese characters on it.

"Jim sent me," I said.

I half expected him to question my sanity. Instead, he nodded, and then disappeared into another room. He came back clutching something which he pressed into my hand.

"You must go now," he told me.

As I returned to my car, I inspected what Chu

had given me. It was a key fob, a remote control of some kind, with two small keys dangling from it.

You might suppose I should have gone to the police with these items, and you'd be right. However, being a journalist, my main concern was to find out if they would lead to a story I could use. I reasoned that I could always bring the police in at a later stage if necessary.

I keyed the 'Old Chapel, Palatine Road' into my GPS and set off through the dark streets.

By the time I reached Didsbury, my destination, night had fallen and the prospect of entering a strange house on my own was far from appealing. I forced myself not to dwell on the dangers and located the Old Chapel. I couldn't see the house itself, only the roof. The rest of it was hidden from view by a high brick wall crowned by metal uprights strung with razor wire. The wooden gates, as high as the wall, were similarly topped off.

On an impulse I pointed the key fob at the gates and pressed the button. They swung smoothly open, closing behind me as I drove through. I proceeded slowly up a gravel drive towards the front of the house, which was, as the name suggested, a converted Victorian chapel set in a tree-lined garden. There were no lights in the garden, but enough illumination entered from the street to reveal windows covered by steel shutters – the sort you install to keep vandals out when you own an empty property.

I left the car and tried one of the keys on the front door. It worked. With the aid of the second key I opened a further lock, went inside, and switched on the lights. Before me lay a grand hall with a tiled floor.

At that stage I experienced a moment of paranoia

and wondered if I might be walking into a trap, so I listened carefully. There was no sound, other than for the creaking of trees in the wind outside. If anyone was already in the house, they were keeping very quiet.

I walked along the hall and entered a room to my left. It contained a desk and chair, and little else.

There was a ledger of some kind on the desk, the journal Jim had been talking about. I couldn't resist dipping into it, and soon enough I got to the bottom of Jim's horrifying secrets.

I don't have the journal to hand, but I know there was a passage that revealed everything. This is what it said, as best as I can piece together from memory:

4

JULY 10

I caught the eye of a young man and smiled at him.
He came over to my table, took hold of my hands with
his, and pulled me to my feet. I went with him
willingly and he led me onto the dance floor, where
he gyrated his hips in front of me.
"I'm going to the bar," I said. "Would you like a
drink?"
"Yes please," he replied. "A bottle of Peroni."
I bought his Peroni and a glass of tonic water for
myself. Before leaving the bar area, I operated the
dispensing device strapped to my wrist and
discharged a small amount of GHB into his drink.
Then I quickly located my new friend.
He grinned as I handed him his Peroni.
"What's your name?" He asked.
That was a question to which I couldn't give an
honest answer. I can imagine the reaction if I did:
"I'm Gabriel, strong man of God, one of the seven
archangels." No, that wouldn't go down at all well.

"Terry," I lied. "But I like to be called Tel. What's
yours?"

"Tel. That's a nice name. I'm Simon. Call me Si."
I nibbled at his ear.

"What are you up to?" he asked, with a big grin on his
face.

"I think you can guess," I said. "Would you like to go
somewhere quieter – my place for example?"

"You don't waste any time. Go on then."

I led him outside. Night had fallen, but the air was
still warm and the street was no less crowded than it
had been an hour or so before when I'd wandered into
the gay village.

"Where are we going?" He asked.

"To my car. I'm parked just round the corner."

"Are you driving me to your plaish?"

He was beginning to slur his speech because of the
combination of alcohol and GHB.

"That's right."

"And what will you do with me when we get there?"

"I'll fuck your brains out."

By the time we got to the Old Chapel, Simon was fast
asleep. With the aid of my specially adapted sack cart
I wheeled him into the house and down the cellar
steps. Then I got him strapped into the chair and
turned the handle of the vice, locking his head into an
upright position in its jaws.

———

JULY 11

I paid him a visit.

"What is this?" He demanded. "Some sick sado-

masochistic game or something? I'm not into anything
like that!"
"I have something here for you to drink," I answered
calmly.
I put a bottle on the table next to him with a long
straw in it that he could just reach with his tongue.
He used his tongue to get the end of the straw in his
mouth and gulped the fluid down eagerly. Then he
looked at me with rage and fear in his eyes.
"Fucking let me out now!" He demanded. "Right
fucking now!"
"If it was up to me, I would," I replied. "But you are in
God's hands. I am His Instrument and He has given
me signs to tell me that you must be purified."
He tried to wriggle his arms and legs free but soon
gave up.

———

JULY 18

I tightened the vice. The massive jaws at either side of
his head moved fractionally closer together.
"What are you doing?" He asked. His voice became
shrill. "What the fuck are you doing?"
I ignored him and carried on with my work.
I took my razor and shaved the top of his head. Then,
using a sharp knife, I cut the shape of a cross in the
bare skin I'd just exposed and peeled it back to reveal
the bone beneath it. When I was satisfied I'd done a
good job, I got my brace and bit from the table and
began drilling a good-sized hole in the top of his head.
His screams as I did this were enough to wake the
dead. When the hole was sufficiently deep, I lit my

incense burner and paced around the cellar swinging it gently, as I chanted the Holy words that would put his Demon to flight.

It was time for the spatula. I used it to scoop out the area of brain tissue in which the Demon had made his home. During this part of the ceremony, Simon somehow found the strength to scream even more loudly than he had done before.

After that, I tightened the jaws of the vice until I heard his skull crack.

Later, I took his body through the tunnel and laid him to rest in the catacombs."

———

END OF EXTRACT FROM JIM'S JOURNAL

5

My god, I thought, *was this some kind of sick fantasy. or has Jim really killed someone-maybe more than one person - in such a vicious and painful way?*

As a conventional family man, I felt horrified by what I was reading.

As a Journalist – I worked for the Manchester Daily News – I must admit that my reaction was rather different. I'm ashamed to admit it, but I found myself actually hoping that Jim might have removed Demons from several 'patients', and that I might be the one to reveal his crimes, by way of an exclusive story.

I cast my mind back to the notes I'd been given about him. He was in prison for the attempted abduction of a young man. It was possible that the police hadn't uncovered the full extent of his criminal activities and it wasn't beyond the bounds of possibility that he was a serial killer, the most prolific in the history of Manchester, or even the U.K.

I looked up from the journal. Two hours had passed very quickly. My eyes were tired and I was beginning to feel I wanted to get home. Moreover, if truth be told, once my mind was no longer occupied by the act of reading, I became concerned for my safety. There is something rather unsettling about being on your own in a strange house late at night.

I decided to make a quick search of the place then get on my way.

There was a stash of Heroin in the kitchen, and, concealed at the rear of an old pantry, a door leading down a flight of steps to a cellar. I decided to take a look. As I descended into the gloom at the bottom of the stairs my instincts screamed at me to leave, but in the interests of journalism I ignored them.

A single naked bulb lit the cellar and the walls were bare brick. There was a crude wooden cupboard in one corner and a faint but lingering smell of incense in the air.

And more.

There was a chair.

It horrified and excited me in equal measure.

The coarse-looking wooden armchair had leather straps with metal buckles on the arms and legs. On top of the back of the chair was a rusting cast-iron vice, its two massive jaws positioned to clamp on either side of the head of anyone sitting in it. A handle much like that of an old fashioned wringing machine could be turned to bring the jaws of the vice together. I cranked the handle: the action felt smooth and powerful.

Nearby sat a wooden table with a cut-throat razor, a knife, and a curved spatula. Next to those items was a brace and bit.

The bit must have been an inch in diameter, and the spatula resembled a spoon with razor sharp edges.

All the tools were caked in dried blood. I didn't have to ask myself why that should be, because I remembered Jim's chilling words.

It seemed the account in his journal wasn't a sick fantasy. It was an accurate record of events that had actually taken place. The discovery set my nerves on edge.

Nevertheless, I examined the chair.

There were spots of dried blood on it and large encrustations of the stuff all over the vice.

I shivered and my knees began to weaken.

I wanted to run away, but I knew that I had to look in the cupboard. Thankfully it contained only shelves, a large number of jars full of pickled cauliflower, and nothing more.

In time I would come to understand the full significance of that cupboard.

But on this, my first visit to the cellar, I was too disorientated with fear to inspect it further.

Having more than satisfied my curiosity, I fled up the steps as fast as I could, ran through the entrance hall, and shot out the front door. Then I breathed deeply, in an effort to calm myself down. With feelings of trepidation, I returned for the journal and took it back to my car.

Finally, and not a moment too soon, I drove back to my home in Chorlton.

It was late when I got there. My wife Sandra was out with her friends and our children were being looked after by a teenage girl who lived down the street. After paying her for her troubles, I began reading Jim's journal, intending to read it from beginning to end and make notes. Although exhausted, I was so excited by what I might find that I managed to keep from nodding off.

Sandra didn't get in until about 2.00 a.m., dressed to the nines, as she usually was on Friday nights when she went out. I glanced in her direction, and saw killer heels and a short skirt.

She never made that effort with me, I reflected sadly. When we were out together, she dressed like a frump. An attractive frump, but a frump nonetheless. The eye-catching makeup she wore tonight was never in evidence when the only person she needed to impress was me.

She said hello, her mobile beeping, so she reached into her bag and looked at it, greeting her new text message with a careful smile.

"Something funny?" I asked.

"Not really," she said, avoiding my eyes.

She went into the kitchen and I heard her pottering around before going upstairs. I went to the kitchen myself to make a coffee, and noticed her bag on the table. A sudden desire seized me to check the messages on her mobile. Some sort of instinct, I suppose. I opened her bag and looked inside. She hadn't left the mobile in it.

I spent another hour perusing Jim's journal before turning in.

I appreciate that I should have gone straight to the police with my findings, but other matters were preying on my mind.

And it may be, that at some subconscious level, I was already contemplating a use for the implements I had found in Jim's cellar.

6

At some time prior to all of this, Sandra had started getting home late from work more frequently. She put it down to a promotion she'd been given which had brought with it more responsibility.

I couldn't help but notice the way she dressed for work had changed in recent months. It was business-like, but sexier than before. I often wondered why she was making such a special effort all of a sudden. I put it down to the need to impress her colleagues. But sometimes I speculated that it might be something else.

Things came to a head the day after I discovered Jim's journals. I went to a pub for a few beers, and Sandra told me she was going out 'with the girls'. These were friends of hers from her University days.

We both got ready, said goodbye to the kids and the babysitter, and went our separate ways. I went to a pub in Manchester's Northern Quarter, and Sandra went God knows where with her youthful friends. She was over twenty years younger than me, and one problem I'd encountered with our age difference was that, in some ways, our worlds were totally different.

I like to go to traditional pubs and enjoy real ale and conversation, mostly about sport and trivia, whereas Sandra enjoys clubbing.

For many years I've gone to the same pubs and bars with the same small group of male friends. On this particular night I was forced to break with tradition because of Mike Rudd, a newcomer amongst our crowd. He'd joined the Manchester Daily News a couple of years before as an Associate Editor. He was forty-five, but thought he was twenty-five.

Rudd dragged us to a combination of club and wine bar. The drinks were overpriced and there was no draught beer, but at least there were places to sit, and I have to admit the scenery, which included a large number of well turned-out young women, was rather eye-catching.

Two of the women in particular caught my eye – Laura and Zoe – the two Sandra was meant to be out with that evening. At least, that's what she'd told me. But there was no sign of Sandra. I wondered if she was in the Ladies. I kept looking towards the corner where the toilets were located, but Sandra didn't appear.

When I got home that night, she was still out, so I read some more of Jim's journal. Eventually I heard Sandra open the front door. She must have noticed I was still up, because she came into the front room. Jenny, the family cat, raised her head lazily to check who it was, and when she saw that it was only Sandra, she settled down for another kip.

"How was your night?" I asked.

I confess my eyes wandered up and down her body, taking in her shape, and her – I couldn't help but use the word in my head – packaging. I have always been an admirer of good packaging on a woman, and Sandra's was better than most. She was wearing a close-fitting silk dress that showed off many of the features I most admired about her, including the tempting valley between her breasts.

"Really good," she replied.

"And how about your friends, how's Laura?" I asked, watching the expression on her face closely.

"She's fine, still at the agency, still enjoying it."

"And Zoe?" Sandra's brow furrowed at this point, but she didn't miss a beat.

"Zoe's still having problems with Clive, but she's happy enough."

Either she was lying to me, or maybe she had been with Laura and Zoe, parting company with them to enjoy a night out with someone else. Either way, she was keeping something from me. But I didn't try to interrogate her; softly, softly catchee monkey.

7

The following Friday I told Sandra that I was going out earlier than usual. I ordered a taxi, took it only as far as the end of our road, then got out and climbed into a parked car. I'd borrowed it from a friend at work and parked it there earlier that day. I jammed a baseball cap on my head, pulling it down so low that it covered my eyebrows, and hoped that this would constitute a disguise of sorts.

Half-an-hour later, a taxi passed by with Sandra in the passenger seat. I pulled out and followed her. Due to my career in journalism I've acquired some basic detective skills, and was able to follow her to her destination without making it too obvious.

It turned out that her destination was a block of flats, the same block where my brother Brian had his apartment. She left the taxi and went inside.

I parked on the opposite side of the street and remained in my car, keeping watch over the entrance.

I sat there for hours but she didn't emerge. Maybe she'd left by a back entrance, or maybe she was in there for the long haul. I had no chance of finding out, as I was busting for a piss and desperate to go home.

I concluded there was a strong possibility that Sandra was having an affair with someone who lived in the same block of flats as Brian, and I determined to find out, one way or another, what was going on.

The following week I met with Jed Barker, the private investigator who worked for the Manchester Daily News on stories requiring professional surveillance.

"Jed," I told him," I need a favour."

He looked up at me from behind his desk, munching on a sandwich. He had a droopy face like a bloodhound and a temperament to match. Once you put him on the trail of something, he'd follow the scent until he'd tracked it down, come what may.

"What is it Brad?" He asked, wiping mayonnaise from his jowls.

"I need you to do some surveillance for me, something a bit different to the usual stuff."

"How different?"

He finished his sandwich, wiped the crumbs from his desk, then licked them from the palm of his beefy hand.

"I'd like you to find out if my wife is having an affair."

He didn't answer immediately. He swallowed the crumbs he'd just put in his mouth, paused, and put his hand to his chin.

"You know I don't do that kind of work, Brad."

That disappointed me. I wanted to use Jed because I knew he was professional and I could rely on him to do a good job. Furthermore, he'd be discreet. I didn't know anybody else who was paid to snoop, and I felt I wouldn't be able to put my trust in a stranger.

I decided to appeal to his better nature – and his self-interest.

"Well, do me a favour, just this once," I said. "Bear in mind that you're happy enough to take on all the jobs I give you from the Manchester Daily News. It won't hurt you to do this extra one for me, even if it's not your usual line of work. And by the way, mate's rates would be appreciated."

Jed took a while to answer. He was probably thinking about all the work I'd put his way over the years, and the catastrophic effect it'd have on his income if I took the MDN account elsewhere.

"All right Brad, you've persuaded me," he said at last.

He took out a pen and notebook.

"What's the background? I'll need addresses, dates, times, and anything else you think might be relevant."

I reeled off all I knew, which was very little. Namely, that Sandra was frequently coming home from work later than she'd done previously, that she might be spending her Friday nights elsewhere than she was letting on, and that her Lothario might occupy the same block of flats as my brother Brian.

"It's a bit thin," he said. "But I'll see what I can do. I'll get onto it this week."

He was as good as his word. Within a matter of days I was in his office again, sitting opposite him at his desk.

"What did you find out, Jed?" I asked.

He didn't reply. Instead, he pushed an A4 brown manila envelope across the desk towards me. I picked it up and examined the contents, a series of photographs taken in a minimalist apartment –

Brian's apartment. My stomach did a somersault. Brian and Sandra – I couldn't believe it.

Brian and Sandra.

Some of those images were tantamount to hard-core pornography. My hands, with the photos in them, began to shake.

"I'm sorry, Brad," said Jed. "I was hoping I wouldn't find anything."

I waited a moment before I replied. I knew it would be hard getting my words past the lump that had formed in my throat.

"Don't worry, it's not as if it's your fault, Jed," I mumbled.

My voice didn't sound like my own.

It was impossible to steady my hands, no matter how hard I tried. Tears welled up in my eyes, but I was brought up old-school, so I suppressed them. I could feel my cheeks getting hot, though.

"How much do I owe you?"

I tried to sound casual, but there was a stress tremor in my voice.

"Nothing, it's on the house," he replied. "Like you said, you give me a lot of work from the MDN. This is my way of repaying the favour."

"Thanks, Jed. You're a star."

I left his office, went straight to the toilets, and threw up everything in my guts. Every last morsel I'd eaten that day, and probably some from the previous day. Then I threw up some more. Weakened with worry and the effort of vomiting, I washed my trembling hands and rinsed out my mouth with clean water.

I made my way to the car park clutching the

23

envelope with the photographs in it, still tasting the vomit in my mouth, and feeling sick.

I got in my car and just sat in it, stomach churning. I don't know how long I stayed there. The news I'd been given was devastating, and I didn't feel like doing anything. It was as if I'd lost the will to live. I couldn't shut my eyes without seeing images of Brian and Sandra in bed together.

Eventually I calmed down enough to make my way home. During the drive I wondered how to handle the situation. Should I confront Sandra? Or have it out with Brian first? What if they both denied everything? If I showed them the photographic evidence, would that concede a portion of the moral high ground to them? Did I really want to let them know I'd been snooping?

I wasn't on remotely good terms with Brian. I'd not got on well with him for a long time. In fact, it's fair to say that my feelings for him verged on hate. There are many good reasons for this. The litany of his sins against me was too long to recite here.

But fucking my wife was the last straw.

No, I decided, I wouldn't be confronting Sandra any time soon, and nor would I be confronting Brian. I would handle this matter by getting even with my brother. That was the way to put matters to rights. And I owed him a lot more than just the traditional beating in a fist-fight.

I felt my hatred of him grow and blossom into something more than hate, something more, even, than loathing. I could not put a name to my new emotion, but whatever it was, it was clean, and pure, and good.

And in the midst of my thoughts of vengeance, an image sprang to mind, uninvited but most welcome.

It was the image of a chair in a dank cold cellar, a chair with straps on it, equipped with a device for crushing skulls.

How interesting it would be, to sit Brian in that chair, and tighten up the jaws of the vice against either side of his repugnant head. I wouldn't have to tighten it up very much; just enough to let him know he couldn't fuck my wife and get away with it.

By the time that I'd pulled up outside my house, I had determined that sooner rather than later, Brian was going to end up in that chair.

8

For the next few days, while I was making my plans for Brian, I tried hard to act normal with Sandra. I didn't entirely succeed. It's hard to act normal with your wife when she's been fucking her brains out with your brother. Every now and again she'd say something like:

"You're very quiet today. Is everything all right?"

And I would reply:

"Of course, everything's fine," with a touch too much cheeriness to be believed.

Then I'd get back to the serious business of planning my act of vengeance.

9

If I am to be honest about things (and circumstances demand that I must be) the problems in my relationship with Sandra were my fault as much as hers, probably more so.

There was, for instance, an incident when we were on a night out together, just the two of us. Something about Sandra's manner had been annoying me all day long. What it was escapes me now, but it must have been important to me at the time.

Anyway, we'd eaten in the Tapas place at the end of Deansgate, and I'd had numerous bottles of premium lager and three quarters of a carafe of wine, and gotten myself into a foul mood. As our night out ended and we made our way to the taxi rank, I began berating her in public. This does not nearly convey the severity of what I did.

I shouted and swore at Sandra to such a degree that two young men came over and enquired as to what was going on and whether she needed their help. They were wily-nilly drawn into our conflict. (When I say 'conflict', that is inaccurate, as you need two to have a conflict, but Sandra wasn't responding to my verbal attack on her. She was doing her best to walk away, with me in hot pursuit).

When I noticed the young men intervening, I shouted at them:

"YOU TWO CAN FUCK RIGHT OFF BEFORE I LEVEL THE FUCKING PAIR OF YER. IT'S NONE OF YOUR FUCKING BUSINESS!"

In retrospect, I can see they were two sterling individuals who only wanted to protect Sandra and to prevent something bad from happening.

A couple of policemen patrolling nearby heard my threats (was there anyone within a quarter mile radius of me who did not hear them?). They took me to one side and explained I would be arrested if I didn't calm down. Sandra got a taxi home, while I remonstrated with the police.

Somehow I avoided arrest and made my own way home in a separate taxi.

The point is that I was older than Sandra, and somewhat irascible. This character defect of mine had not improved with age. On the contrary, it had gotten worse. When I wasn't being impatient with Sandra, I was losing my temper with her. I can see why, over the years, she'd gradually withdrawn from our relationship.

But what I still fail to see is why Brian should have taken it on himself to occupy the void created by my absence from certain areas of Sandra's life.

Is it any wonder that I wanted to bring him to book for his treachery?

10

Before I'd be able to provide Brian with the lesson that he so richly deserved, I needed to learn a few lessons myself.

I needed to know where I could get hold of the drug GHB, how much to use, how to discreetly spike the victim's drink, and so on. So I read certain sections of Jim's journal to familiarise myself with his method of preparing his victims (or patients, as he called them) for Exorcism.

Luckily for me, Jim had researched the effects of the drug and drawn up tables that provided the amounts required to sedate men, women and children (*children!*) His journal indicated how the amount should be varied in accordance with the weight of the subject. I read the information over and over again.

His data stood me in good stead. I knew how much Sandra weighed, and I had a good idea how much Brian weighed. Jim's files told me everything else I needed to know.

There were a number of bottles at the Old Chapel containing a liquid that matched Jim's description of the drug. I took one of them home, mashed up a tin of Tuna, and mixed in a drop or two of the liquid that the bottle contained. I gave it to Jenny, the family cat. This was a safety measure: I didn't want to risk killing Brian or Sandra with the drug and I reasoned that if Jenny could survive it, Brian and Sandra would.

Jenny loved Tuna but she smelt the doctored batch and turned to walk away. Then she changed her mind and nibbled around the edges of her food bowl, trying to avoid the contaminated bits. After a minute or two she left the kitchen, having ignored most of the meal I had so carefully prepared for her. I threw it in the bin to make sure that Jack didn't eat any of it. He was only three years old and had been known to eat cat food in his time.

About ten minutes later, my daughter Lucy ran up to me with tears in her eyes.

"Daddy!" She shouted. "Come quick! You've got to help! Jenny's dying!"

I followed Lucy to the front room where Jenny lay asleep in front of the fire, a deeply worried Jack sitting next to her. Sandra was out, probably at Brian's flat, I reflected bitterly.

"Look Daddy!" Said Lucy.

She shook Jenny, who refused to stir. The cat just lay there with her body gently rising and falling in time with her breathing. I looked at Jenny and felt worried sick. I'm a cat-lover and Jenny was a cat I loved dearly.

"Don't worry Lucy, I'm sure it's nothing serious," I told her, with a confidence that I didn't feel. "I'm sure she'll be all right."

Lucy looked up at me with big sad eyes.

"Aren't you going to take her to the Vet, Daddy?" She asked.

That was the very last thing I wanted to do. What if the Vet was able to tell that someone had poisoned Jenny? How would I explain it?

"I don't think so," I said. "She's probably just sleeping. Let's wait and see how she gets on."

I forced myself to give the kids a reassuring smile but I was as troubled as they were. Our family cat had been a great source of comfort to me during Sandra's many absences. I hoped to God that I hadn't done her a serious mischief.

"You two can go and play. Don't worry about Jenny. I'll look after her," I said.

I felt like Judas. It was heart rending.

When the kids had left, I knelt next to Jenny and cradled her little furry head in my hand. Her neck was limp, and her body seemed lifeless other than for her quiet breathing. I gently placed her head back on the carpet, and sat in the front room watching over her. I tried to pass the time by reading a book, but couldn't focus enough to get beyond the first paragraph.

After a couple of hours, she yawned and stretched out her front legs. Then she washed herself and went into the kitchen looking for the rest of the Tuna, which, thankfully, I had disposed of. I picked her up and she looked pissed off, as she always did when I manhandled her. Then she struggled, so I returned her to the kitchen floor and she shot me a look that said:

"Fuck the cuddles, I want to be fed. Now."

I knew better than to dally, so I opened a tin of

Sheba (a premium cat food – she never ate anything less) and left her stuffing her face.

So, Jenny the cat had made a full recovery.

That was a welcome development.

Most promising.

It was all systems go.

I had to devote a few distasteful weeks to preparing the ground with Brian.

If he was to be willing to meet with me late at night at short notice (which is what my plan required) he would have to believe that, after all of our ups and downs over the years, we were finally on a prolonged up. So I made a point of spending time with him, and being nice to him. It was most painful for me, but it was all in a good cause, I told myself.

I put my plan into action on a night when the kids were having a sleepover at someone's house, a friend's birthday party or something.

At bedtime I poured myself a nightcap and offered to get one for Sandra. She asked for a small whiskey, which I provided, laced with a few drops of Jim's GHB. The dosage was calculated to ensure that she would enjoy the benefits of a full night's sleep.

Sandra soon nodded off. When she did, I climbed out of bed and got dressed. That was the way it had to be, she couldn't know anything about my movements from that point on. What I had in mind for Brian amounted to abduction, false imprisonment, and assault. If he was to go to the police about it, I wanted to have an alibi – and Sandra would provide me with one, if I played my cards right. She would testify that we'd gone to bed early and had spent the entire night in bed together. That was the theory, anyway.

It was about 10.00 p.m. when I drove over to Brian's place. Sandra and I tend to get to bed early during the week, but Brian would still be up and about. He worked as an IT consultant, and as he didn't have to get up at the crack of dawn to sort out children, he enjoyed the luxury of staying up late every night.

I parked out of sight around a corner, went to the entrance of his block of flats, and rang the bell. I was wearing a Hoodie with the hood up, and I kept my head bowed so if the security cameras filmed me, it wouldn't be possible to identify me.

Brian answered, and when I told him who it was, he buzzed me inside. I took the lift to his floor. When I got there he was waiting at his door, which was open. He showed me inside.

It pained me to admit it, but he was good-looking in a dated 50s movie-star kind of way, and had the toned body of an athlete. He'd looked after himself. The bastard.

"Brian," I said, "I feel awful. I've got the most terrible problem. I've got to talk to you. It's really important."

I had a bottle of whiskey in my hand.

"It must be if it can't wait till tomorrow," he observed sneeringly.

But I noticed him looking with interest at the whiskey, and inspecting the label on the bottle. It was

Monkey Shoulder, a brand to which I knew he was most partial.

"I'll pour us both a drink," I said. "I need a drink."

His face lit up with anticipation.

"You know where the glasses are."

He had a galley kitchen to one side of his sitting room. I took two glasses from a cupboard and poured us both a generous measure. With my back to him covering my movements, I tipped a small measure of GHB into the glass I'd earmarked for him. Then I went to where he was sitting and handed him his glass.

"So what's this all about, Brad?" He asked.

I did my best to look tearful. It wasn't difficult. All I had to do was to think of Brian in bed with Sandra.

"I'm in a state Brian, and I need your advice," I said.

He assumed a sage-like air of importance. It was a bad habit of his.

"I'll do my best," he said. "Just tell me what's bothering you. I'll give you my honest opinion on what you should do. I'm usually pretty good at that sort of thing."

"It's Sandra," I told him. "I'm worried she's having an affair and I'm in bits about it. I just don't know what to do."

For an instant he looked concerned and guilty. He was probably worried that I might be onto him.

"It's the way she's been behaving," I continued. "She hasn't been herself for a while now. I don't have anything to go on, as such, but I know she's seeing someone else. You can have an instinct for these things."

My faux-naïve manner completely took him in.

He lost his worried look. It was replaced with something akin to triumph, which he immediately suppressed in favour of an expression he perhaps thought approximated to brotherly concern.

"That must be awful, Brad. You and Sandra have always seemed rock solid to me. I find it hard to believe she'd cheat on you. Can you really be sure about it?"

"I'm sure. And I need to talk about it. I need to get it off my chest."

He put his glass to his lips and took a sip from it. He hadn't imbibed nearly enough for my purposes, but still, I felt like cheering.

"Well, I'm here for you, Brad," he assured me. "You know you can talk to me."

I took large gulp of my own whiskey in the hope it might encourage him to do the same.

"Yes, I know I can Brian," I responded. "The last few weeks have shown me that you're a friend I can depend on as well as a brother. I can't believe we've spent just most of our adult lives not talking to one another. I'm glad we've got over that, because I don't know who else I could have told about this."

He drained his glass, putting it down with a smug expression on his face. I began to top it up for him, but saw his eyelids droop and knew a further drink wouldn't be necessary.

"Brian," I said. "BRIAN!"

He didn't answer. He just sat there, somewhere between sleep and wakefulness, exactly as I'd planned.

I hauled him to his feet and marched him to the door. He came along willingly, had no strength to resist, indeed, no will to resist. He was like a drunk, but lacked the truculence of the average drunk. Anyone who saw us probably thought he was at the end of an eight hour bender, and I was helping him get home, whereas I was doing the very opposite.

We left the building together, Brian the drunk with an unidentifiable male wearing a Hoodie. I held him tenderly, as if to ensure that he wouldn't lose his footing. We turned the corner safely out of sight of the security cameras (I had checked) and got into my car.

Well, Brian didn't exactly get in; I pushed him into the passenger side. It wasn't easy, even though he was quite compliant. He was tall, muscular, and heavy, so I had quite a struggle, but eventually I got him where I wanted and fastened his seatbelt for him.

I drove to the Old Chapel, opened the gates with my remote fob, and manoeuvred my car smartly through. Brian peered at the eerie surroundings through the side window next to him. He didn't say anything, his jaw too slack for speech by that stage.

I dragged him out of the car as carefully as I could, not wanting to injure him, and walked him into the house.

By this time he was on the verge of sleep. When I lowered him onto a sofa he shut his eyes. Minutes later he was snoring like a well-fed pig.

My brother weighed in at around 210 pounds because of his big muscles, and it would have been a huge effort for me to move him unassisted to the cellar and strap him into the chair waiting for him. It was a job that would have taxed the efforts of two burly men. But Jim's modified sack cart made matters relatively straightforward. One feature it had puzzled me: it had four wheels, two of which appeared to be redundant.

Getting Brian on it was a struggle, but once I'd got him securely strapped in, getting him down to the cellar was a relatively easy matter. I struggled to transfer his limp body to the chair, and by the time I'd done that, I was puffing and panting with the effort of it all. But I felt it was going to be worth it.

I secured his arms and legs to those of the chair, making sure the buckles on the leather straps were done up good and tight. Then I turned the handle of the vice until the jaws clamped firmly against either side of his head. All that effort was tiring so I left the cellar and took a much-needed rest for a while. On my return, I filled a bucket with ice-cold water and hurled it against his face. It made a satisfying splash, just like it does in the movies. He opened his eyes and stared uncertainly at me through the gloom.

"Where am I?" He asked. "What's going on?"

For once, there was no sneer on his face as he spoke to me. I had waited a long time for this and was minded to relish every second of it.

"You are in a dark cellar," I told him. "You are unable to move, and you are completely at my mercy. You are strapped to a piece of apparatus that can be used to inflict extreme pain and suffering, and even death if I choose. I think that about sums it up."

He tried to move his limbs, but they were held tight by the restraints.

I paced back and forth in front of him, reminding myself of what he had done to me, and working myself up into a fine state of fury. His eyeballs danced right, then left, then right again, tracking my movements, but his head remained stationary, trapped, as it was, in the pitiless jaws of the vice.

Brian appreciated the gravity of his predicament remarkably quickly.

"Brad, please, let me go," he implored.

There was a stress tremor in his voice, as well there might be.

"I don't propose letting you go for a long time," I told him.

This wasn't true. I said it just to scare him. In fact, I thought I might keep him prisoner for only a couple of hours – just long enough to make him see the error of his ways and regret them – then set him free.

"Come on, Brad," he pleaded. "Let me out. Why are you doing this?"

I stopped my pacing.

"Because of you," I told him, pointing my right index finger directly at his face. It shook with rage as I pointed. I wondered if he noticed that.

"I'm doing it because of you. It's entirely your

own fault that you're stuck in that chair. Deep down, you know that. Did you never stop to remind yourself that Hubris is often followed by Nemesis?"

These were words that in time would come back to haunt me.

His forehead wrinkled.

"What do you mean?" He sounded genuinely puzzled.

I wagged my finger at him.

"You know what I mean."

"I don't, I promise you Brad, I have no idea why you're doing this."

I bent down so my head was at the same level as his and stuck my face up close to his so that our noses were only an inch or so apart.

"BECAUSE YOU'VE BEEN FUCKING MY WIFE THAT'S WHY!!!!" I shouted.

His eyes grew to the size of dinner plates.

"No, I haven't, honest, I don't know what you're talking about," he claimed.

He was a good liar, I'll give him that.

I straightened up.

"You don't, eh? Then let me help you to get a better understanding," I said.

Taking the brown envelope Jed Barker had given me I slid out the photographic evidence of Brian's most recent crimes against me. I held the pictures in front of his face one by one. He had no choice other than to look at them. He couldn't turn his head away.

"You were saying?" I asked.

It was hard to tell in the gloom of the cellar, but I believe he may have reddened.

"All right," he said. He sounded more than a little tense by this stage. Had he known what lay in store for him, he would have been beside himself. "I'll admit it, you're right. Sandra and I have been seeing each other. We've been sleeping together. But it isn't my fault. She was the one who started it. She came on to me, and I couldn't resist. You know what she's like. She's beautiful and determined, and she always gets what she wants. I couldn't help myself."

It was my turn to sneer.

"How noble you are," I replied, "trying your level best to save your own miserable hide, by heaping all the blame on Sandra. I must say that your behaviour is everything I expected of you, and more. I find your excuse that you 'couldn't help yourself' pitiful beyond words. All you had to do was to keep your dick in your pants."

His voice went an octave higher.

"I tried to do that Brad, I promise. I turned her down, but she wouldn't take 'no' for an answer. I had to be talked into it. I was practically forced into it. You know what she's like. I couldn't stand up to her."

I shook my head in mock sympathy.

"I'm truly sorry that you were subjected to such hideous pressure, Brian. The realization that you had no option other than to fuck my wife must have come as a terrible blow."

"Brad, please listen to me, I didn't make the first move."

I stuck my face up close to his again.

"Whether you made the first move or not is immaterial," I hissed.

"What are you going to do to?" He whined.

"I'm going to teach you a lesson. A very painful one."

I took hold of the handle operating the vice and

gave it a little bit of a turn. Although the vice was rusty, Jim had taken care to ensure that all the moving parts had been kept well greased. The jaws moved smoothly towards each other, tightening their grip around Brian's head. He screamed. I loosened them off a little. There was, I noticed, a growing dark patch at the crutch of his trousers.

"How was that?" I asked. "Have you got the message yet? If you're still unclear about what the message is, I'll tell you in plain words: it's that you don't fuck with my wife and you don't fuck with me!"

"YES!" He shouted. "YES, YES, I'VE GOT THE MESSAGE! Please don't do that again!"

His response was a little too quick and glib for my liking, not well considered, and probably not entirely sincere. It was not half as satisfying for me as it should have been, so I decided to give him another little taste of what the vice could do.

"I'm going to tighten this mother up until you beg me to stop," I said quietly.

"Brad," he pleaded, "you don't have to do that. I'm begging you now. I'm already begging you to stop. PLEASE STOP! FOR PITY'S SAKE PLEASE LET ME OUT NOW!!!"

"Nice try, Brian," I told him. "But I'm afraid I've already made up my mind."

I cranked the handle and he began screaming again. It was music to my ears. So much so that I cranked it some more.

I knew that I'd gone too far when an eyeball popped out of its socket with a sort of liquid plop. It dangled at the end of the optic nerve, wobbling near the top of Brian's right cheek. It seemed to be looking at me accusingly. I hadn't expected that. I wondered what I should do.

Then it came to me quite clearly.

I reached for the brace and bit.

13

I stuck the bit on top of Brian's cranium, applied pressure, and began turning the brace. He was still screaming.

"WHAT ARE YOU DOING? NO! OH MY FUCKING GOD NO!!!"

For a moment I felt a scintilla of pity for Brian and thought about letting him go. But then I remembered I hated him, and that he had been fucking my wife, and I pressed on with renewed vigour.

Brian had lank brown hair that soon got tangled up in the bit. Then a large portion of his hair and scalp seemed to cling to the bit and rotate with it. At first I was puzzled by this development, but soon I realised that Brian was wearing a wig. This was something I hadn't expected. I wondered how come I'd never noticed it before, and whether Sandra had known about it. But in some ways I wasn't surprised by my discovery. It was in keeping with everything about my brother. He was one of life's fakes.

I removed the wig from the bit and hurled it into a

corner of the cellar, where it lay unmoving and unloved, like a dead rat.

Without the wig to protect it, Brian's exposed bald pate looked strangely vulnerable. It had a small hole in the middle of it where the tool had just begun to penetrate. I stuck the point of the bit into the hole and turned the brace once again. It rucked up the skin on the top of Brian's head, then began to slice through it. After a few seconds I felt it biting into his skull. It was a strangely pleasurable feeling as I watched it churn up pieces of white bone, along with blood and assorted gore from an increasingly large cavity. At one point, a fountain of blood splashed across my face like an oil gusher. I hoped it hadn't stained my clothes.

I'd never used a brace and bit before, and found it hard going. This was partly because the bit had been used many times and was rather blunt, and partly because of the waves of emotion sweeping over me, draining my energy. My chest heaved and the strength soon left my arms. I took a brief respite, as I didn't want to compromise the quality of the job by working in a state of fatigue. When I'd recovered, I continued.

After I had made what I judged to be an adequately sized aperture, I stepped back to check my handiwork. It looked good.

Next came the finishing touch.

I took Jim's spatula – the one he used specifically for this purpose – and scooped out a decent amount of fresh brain tissue. It steamed gently in the cold air of the cellar. Brian might have stopped screaming at that stage, but I'm not sure.

I made a point of removing sufficient tissue to well and truly liberate any Demons that might have been lurking in Brian's body. I wanted my patient to be fully cured of his malaise. I think I can safely say that he was.

After that, I wasn't sure what I should do. The original plan hadn't called for my brother to be killed, and I felt a little bit flustered by the turn of events, but I was too tired and emotionally drained to deal with it.

I decided to leave him where he was for the time being, clean myself up, and go home.

14

When I sneaked back into bed with Sandra, she didn't stir. As usual, I put my head on the pillow and tried to relax. But as soon as I shut my eyes, my head was filled with ghastly images. I did my best to ignore them and after an hour or two fell into a fitful sleep.

In the one and only dream I had that night, I was talking to Brian at my parents' house. We were all sitting in the front room enjoying a mug of tea. My brother was holding forth about his short stories. He fancied himself as a brilliant polymath who was better than me at everything – particularly writing – and he never let me forget it.

It was a normal family scene, or it would have been, were it not for the fact that one of Brian's eyes dangled out of its socket. It rolled around his face and stared at me every time he turned his head. He and my parents seemed unaware that there was anything amiss.

The following morning I woke up feeling distinctly out of sorts. I told myself it had just been a bad dream, and looked forward to a normal day at work.

Then the recollection of what I had done the previous night hit me like a pile-driver in the stomach and sweat erupted from the palms of my hands. As I lay there in a state of shock, Sandra rolled over, and said:

"I don't know what sort of whiskey you gave me last night, but it was bloody marvellous. I've never felt better."

I did my best to respond as I would have done on any normal day.

"It was just the usual. Grants blended," I told her. "It must have been the way I poured it."

She looked at me and narrowed her eyes.

"Are you coming down with something?" She asked. "You sound as if you have a sore throat."

My throat wasn't sore, it was dry and parched with anxiety, and possibly from screaming at Brian.

"I'm all right," I croaked. "I just need a drink of water, that's all."

With some difficulty due to my jangling nerves, I got out of bed, showered, and fumbled myself into my clothes. It gave me an unwelcome insight into what people mean when they describe an experience as "a living nightmare".

When I got to the office, I did my best to avoid any thoughts about Brian and what I'd done to him. But in spite of my efforts, I couldn't keep it from my mind. My hands shook and I was unable to concentrate on my job. It was as if I was a lightning conductor and anxiety was crackling through the ether. I also felt guilty, but that was far from the greatest of my concerns.

If truth be known, my first concern was that I might be caught and locked up for murder.

My second was that the kids would grow up thinking that their Dad was a Freak.

My third was that my parents would never forgive me.

Guilt was, at best, my fourth concern, very far behind the three main ones. And I confess, I wasn't remotely bothered about what Sandra might think of me. That didn't even begin to register.

I realised that I had to find a way to dispose of Brian's body. It wasn't safe to leave it in that cellar for too long. Someone could break in at any time and happen upon the evidence of my crime.

I made an excuse, left the office, and went to an out-of-town Builders Merchants. Before I got out of my car I put on my Hoodie with the hood up. Then I went inside and furtively bought some tarpaulin and concrete blocks, a length of heavy-duty chain, and a few other items, for which I paid cash.

I hoped I looked like a builder buying supplies for his trade, but I probably looked more like a serial killer buying the provisions he needed to dispose of a body. Fortunately the girl at the checkout didn't notice anything suspicious.

That evening I told Sandra I had to go out to investigate a promising lead for a story and drove back to the Old Chapel.

Brian was still where I'd left him, in the chair with his eye hanging out and a crater like a small volcano on the top of his head. His mouth was wide open, and all-in-all he didn't look too happy. I knew just how he felt.

I donned a pair of rubber gloves and pulled him

from the chair. He didn't get out of it willingly; rigor mortis had set in and he was stiff as a statue. It was impossible to work with him in that condition, so I took a lump hammer and whacked one of his knees with it. It made a splintering sound like dry wood snapping and after that the knee became more obliging. I applied the same treatment to all Brian's major joints.

When he was sufficiently flexible to manipulate, I put him on the tarpaulin and stripped off his clothes, stuffing them into a black bin liner. I put some surgical spirit in a bucket and carefully washed him all over with a sponge, hoping to remove any DNA evidence of my contact with him. Then I rolled him in the tarpaulin and secured him to the sack cart.

Dragging him up the cellar steps was hard going, even with the aid of the sack cart. It made me wonder how Jim had managed it. The job nearly finished me off. When I reached the top of the stairs my heart was pounding like a jackhammer – so much so that I feared I might succumb to a heart attack. I pushed him into a corner of the pantry and sat down. It took a while for me to feel normal. When I did, I realised it was too late to get rid of the body and, even if it hadn't been, I was too traumatised to deal with it. I had to take time out to recover my composure, no matter what the risk was of leaving Brian in the house. So I wiped the sweat from my brow and drove home.

I spent the next few days in a sort of dream state. Logic dictated that I should have returned to the Old Chapel as soon as possible and got rid of the evidence of my crime, but I didn't. I simply couldn't bring myself to face what I'd done. On numerous occasions I tried to imagine it had all been a very bad dream, but that was a fiction I couldn't make myself swallow for long.

I don't remember how many days passed with Brian in the pantry on the sack cart, and me wandering around in a daze refusing to do what it was necessary to do. What I do recall is that by the time I was able to pull myself together sufficiently to do the job, Brian was decomposing somewhat. I knew this even before I saw him because of the foul stench coming from the tarpaulin he was wrapped up in.

Anyway, after telling one of my growing number of lies to my wife, I left the house late at night, got my brother, put him and his bag of clothes into the back of my car, and headed out along the Alderley road. Somewhere on that road was a turning onto a muddy track leading through a copse of trees to a disused quarry. It would make the perfect hiding place. But in the darkness of night, it was hard for me to locate the turning. After driving past it a few times, I finally saw it and made my way slowly up the track, with the car pitching and rolling over the many potholes along the way.

One of them was so deep and muddy that the car, once in, could not get out, and came to a juddering halt. I took my foot off the accelerator and pressed it again, but it was no use. The car wouldn't budge. The rear wheels found no traction, and all they did was churn up more mud.

I got out feeling something close to dread. What if my car was stuck and I couldn't get it to move? While suppressing that negative thought and one or two others (such as: what if a police car should come driving into the woods late at night?), I inspected the rear wheels with the aid of my torch.

The pothole I'd got trapped in was abnormally deep. This track had never been meant for cars. It was going to be touch and go.

There was a spare tarpaulin in the back of my car. I rammed it beneath one of the wheels as best I could. Then I gathered up some brushwood and packed it under the other wheel. After that, I got back in the car and said a little prayer to a God I no longer believed in, and I pressed the accelerator pedal.

The car lurched forwards to freedom.

Thank you, God.

As soon as the vehicle was on a level surface, I applied the brakes, stopped it, got out, and gathered up the tarpaulin.

I drove further along the track to where it emerged from the trees and manoeuvred as close as I dared get to the quarry just beyond them. I ended up parked close to the edge of a precipice. Just a few feet ahead was a vertical drop of a hundred feet or more into a deep lagoon that filled the bottom of the quarry.

I got out and removed Brian from the back of my car. It took a mighty heave. He landed in the dirt with a meaty thud. It was lucky I had an estate car that allowed me to drag him out. I couldn't have hauled him up over the lip of a boot. I pushed him up near the edge of the precipice and unrolled the tarpaulin. The darkness was most welcome – it meant I didn't have to look at him. I secured the concrete blocks to his feet with the chain. Finally, I pushed Brian over the edge and waited for the splash.

It never came.

Instead, an almighty bang resounded around the bare stone walls of the quarry for several seconds. It sounded as if someone had let off a stick of dynamite.

It was enough to wake the dead. I wondered how many people might have heard it and might even now be rushing to the quarry to find out what had caused it.

I couldn't understand what had gone wrong. I looked over the edge, but it was too dark to see anything. I tried using my torch but it wasn't powerful enough to penetrate that far through the gloom, so I walked around the lip of the quarry and found a path down to the bottom. Once I'd descended to the level of the lagoon, I was able, with the aid of my torch, to see what had happened. For some reason there was a wooden platform in the water at the base of the rockface. It was about eight feet square. By the most unfortunate coincidence, Brian had landed on the platform. I cursed myself for failing to investigate the area thoroughly before putting my plan into operation.

I considered what I should do. I couldn't leave Brian lying there in the open. As soon as daylight came, the first person to walk his dog around the quarry would see him. There was nothing for it. I'd have to swim out to the wooden platform and get Brian off it and into the water. It was a prospect that filled me with dread.

I removed my clothes and waded into the lagoon. It became deep surprisingly quickly, the water black and icy cold. It was a moonless night, and there was not even starlight to see by, owing to the cloud cover. The only relief from the darkness was the feeble beam of my torch, which I gripped between my teeth as I swam. I prayed to God that I wouldn't drop it.

I made my way across the lagoon to the wooden platform, a distance of about fifty feet. It took everything I had in me to get there, owing to my age, my lack of physical fitness, and the need to hold my head up high so as to keep the torch out of the water. Somehow I reached the platform without drowning myself and hauled myself onto it. My arms are not very strong in relation to my weight and it took me several attempts. Finally, I managed. I was so drained by the effort that I didn't have the strength to stand up; the best I could manage was to roll over and lay on my back, gasping like a landed fish. I knew that if it had been daylight I would have been able to see the considerable mound of my own stomach rising and falling swiftly in time to my laboured breathing.

I lay there for a long time, barely able to think, let alone move. I was weak and desperately unfit.

I'd been on exercise programs many times over the years and given them all up within a few weeks or months. Every New Year had brought with it a fresh resolution that this was the year I finally did something about my physical condition, but I had never followed through. As I lay on the platform getting my breath back, I swore to myself that I would finally do something to re-invigorate the flabby travesty that my body had become.

At length I was able to get on my hands and knees and start pushing Brian towards the edge of the platform. It wasn't easy. The thing was made of coarse planks and there was a lot of friction. His skin kept catching on splinters and he got stuck on some bent nails that were sticking up like fishhooks.

In desperation, I got to my feet, picked up the concrete blocks that were tied to his feet with the chain, and tossed them into the water, one at a time. I hoped that the weight of them might pull Brian off the platform, but it didn't. He was too heavy, and he was stuck fast to those blasted nails. I got back to pushing him.

Somehow, when all seemed lost, I rolled him off the platform with a desperate shove.

He broke the still water with a gentle splash and sank like a stricken ship, disappearing swiftly beneath the dark undulating surface.

I sat back on my haunches and breathed a sigh of relief. Then I shone my torch on the area of the lagoon where Brian had gone under to make sure he was gone for good.

He wasn't.

To my horror, he rose slowly back up, until his head stuck out above the gently rippling surface. I directed the beam of my torch directly at him; he returned my gaze with one sad eye. The other, the one that had been dangling out of the socket, seemed to be missing. I shone my torch around the platform looking for it, but I couldn't find it. I prayed it hadn't dropped out into my car and made a mental note to search all the nooks and crannies in the back of it when I got home.

I reached out and tried pushing his head underwater, but it kept bobbing up again. The lagoon can't have been as deep as I'd imagined it to be. The concrete blocks must have been resting on the bottom, and Brian must have been trailing at the end of the chain that connected him to the blocks. He was like a ship at anchor, or a buoy.

I realised that I would have to leave him where he was. It was too risky to stay there any longer and possibly draw attention to the body.

I swam sadly back to shore and donned my

clothes. Next I found a suitable spot in the woods and dug a hole with a spade, put the bag of Brian's clothes in it, and burnt them. For good measure, I buried them after they'd finished burning. Then I headed home, feeling defeated and depressed.

Because I hadn't been able to dry myself, my feet squelched uncomfortably in my shoes as I operated the pedals of my car. It somehow reminded me of some of the things I'd done to Brian.

By the time I got back, Sandra had put the kids to bed. I wanted to avoid seeing her until I'd sorted myself out, but I bumped into her in the hallway without getting the opportunity to flee upstairs to safety.

"What's happened to you?" She asked. "You look like you've been dragged backwards through a hedge."

"Nothing. It's been a trying day."

You don't know the half of it, I thought. Luckily, I'd just about dried out by then, and she didn't notice the squelching sound my shoes were making. I suppose at the time she didn't have much interest in anything I might do, so squelching shoes didn't register on the Bitch Radar – although the noise of it seemed impossibly loud to me.

When Sandra was out of the way, I went to the bathroom and locked myself in. I stripped off and inspected myself in the bathroom mirror. I was covered in grime from the wooden platform, which the dirty water of the lagoon had done nothing to remove, and my feet were black bright from the mud that had entered my shoes. Worse, my knees were red raw from crawling about butt naked on rough wood while trying to push my brother into the water and my hands were almost as bad.

I knew then I had left a wealth of forensic evidence in the quarry. My skin and DNA would be all over the wooden platform; my footprints would be everywhere; and there would be incriminating tyre tracks leading up to the precipice from which I had thrown Brian.

To cap it all, I'd left him sticking up out of the water like a beacon sending out a signal that proclaimed "Arrest Brad – he did this to me!"

I knew I'd have to go back soon, and somehow get rid of the evidence.

But I couldn't go back to the quarry that evening. I couldn't face it again, not so soon after the first time, and besides, I needed a plan.

I put my shoes and clothes in a plastic carrier bag I'd smuggled upstairs and rammed them out of sight in the back of my wardrobe. Then I took a shower and got my jammies on.

I poured myself a generous tumbler of whiskey and tried to relax, but that was impossible as I had the jitters. My hands were shaking so much that my ice cubes rattled against the sides of the glass. I had to remove them, as I didn't want Sandra to notice that I was in any way out of sorts.

I knew that it was only a matter of time before Brian's body would be discovered, and then the police would come knocking. Sandra would put two and two together, and that would be that.

I turned in, but couldn't sleep. My mind was racing, thinking about all the evidence that might incriminate me and working out ways of getting rid of it. During the night I might have slept for a total of ten minutes, most of which were spent dreaming about Brian staring at me accusingly through the empty socket that had once been an eye.

During the night Sandra said crossly:

"You're tossing and turning so much I haven't had a wink of sleep. Try to keep still. What's the matter with you?"

"Nothing. Just thinking about a story. I shouldn't bring my work home with me, sorry. 'Night."

Sandra was right, though. I'd been spinning like a top.

The next day I told Sandra that I was feeling under the weather, then called in sick at work. I took some glass bottles out of our recycling bin, drove a few miles, and parked near a petrol station. I bought a plastic petrol carrier and filled it with petrol. As before, I wore my hoodie with the hood up as I made my purchase.

Then I headed back to the quarry. Going back there was a high-risk strategy but I felt I had no choice. If I didn't return to clear up the mess I'd made, there would be more than enough evidence to put me behind bars for a long time.

15

The drive to the quarry seemed to take forever. My heart was pounding so loudly I thought I could actually hear it above the sound of the engine. I played some rock music to drown out the noise of it, but it didn't work.

When I reached my destination, I checked to make sure no-one else was around. In the morning light, the quarry was no less eerie than it had been in the darkness. But at least the place was deserted. I'd half expected it to be swarming with police.

I looked over the precipice. Brian was close to the vertical rock face, still bobbing in the water. I hoped that no-one had been out there before me and noticed him. If they had, the police would be on their way and I'd be arrested in the act of covering my tracks.

The first part of my plan called for destroying any DNA evidence that might be lurking on the wooden platform. I made up some Molotov cocktails and dropped them over the edge of the precipice directly onto it. The first one landed in the middle, then bounced off into the water. The second fared much better. It exploded, creating a savagely roaring ball of flame. The next three Molotov cocktails detonated near it, doing the same. Soon the wooden platform burned fiercely, sending a pall of smoke spiralling up the face of the drop. Brian was close enough to the inferno to have his hair singed by the heat, but he appeared to be nonchalantly taking a dip in spite of the risk.

This would presumably remove all trace of my skin and DNA from the crime scene. But it would do nothing to conceal my footprints. I would just have to throw away the incriminating shoes I'd worn on the night in question. The fact that the murderer might have the same shoe size as me could easily be explained away as coincidence.

It occurred to me that I ought to try and get Brian safely underwater, but I wasn't sure how to go about it. I couldn't swim out to him carrying anything to weigh him down, as anything heavy would weigh me down too much to swim with it. As a result of my experience the previous evening, I knew just how feeble my swimming was. The best I could think of was to throw rocks from the edge of the cliff and hope that one of them would land on Brian and sink him.

There were quite a few good-sized rocks lying around. I lobbed one over the edge and it came close to Brian's head, but didn't score a direct hit on him. I threw over a few more which missed, then finally I caught him square-on with a veritable boulder. It didn't make any difference. He bobbed under for a few moments then annoyingly bobbed up again.

I felt depressed. I was ashamed of myself. This was the most inept attempt to conceal a body in criminal history.

I should have done better. My background demanded that I do better.

After leaving school I'd studied Criminology at the Manchester Metropolitan University (or Polythechnic, as it was then) and emerged at the age of 21 with a 2.1 degree with Honours. Then I went to a specialist college to study Journalism. When I'd qualified, I joined the Manchester Daily News, where I had, since the age of thirty, been their Crime Reporter. That made a total of thirty-two years of theoretical experience in crime, if you included my years spent studying on the degree course.

Why was I so bad at putting the theory into practice?

I was behaving like a rank amateur.

That's the problem when decent people like me get drawn into behaving like criminals. We don't have any talent for it and we don't really know what we're doing. It always ends up messy.

I gave up on the boulder idea and told myself I had to think the matter through. I breathed deeply and used meditation techniques I'd learnt at Sandra's birthing classes to calm myself down. And I asked myself: *what would the villains I've written about do in a situation like this?*

That helped me to come up with an idea. During the course of my reporting career, I'd heard that bodies can become buoyant due to the gasses they contain. If I could get rid of the gasses, maybe Brian would sink.

I took a screwdriver from my car and hurried down to the water's edge. I knew I had to act quickly. Sooner or later, someone would come for a walk around the quarry and I didn't want them catching me at work. I undressed and for the second time in twelve hours, swam across the lagoon. I wished I'd thought of this before setting fire to the wooden platform, because the temperature made it difficult for me to get near enough to Brian to carry out my plan. I had to dive under the water to avoid the fierce heat while still a few yards from him. Before I did, I took some deep breaths, filling my nose and mouth with the stench of petrol and singed hair. Somehow I stopped myself from heaving and swam beneath the surface to the point where my brother was bobbing at anchor.

I plunged the screwdriver several times into his bloated belly and his broad back. Bubbles came out of the punctures and he lost his buoyancy. As he sank, he placed his repugnant hands on my shoulders and began to drag me down with him.

I caught my foot in the chain that connected Brian's ankles to the concrete blocks and we hit the bottom of the lagoon together. I found myself beneath him and wrestled desperately to break free of his grasp. It was a fight to the finish. The tables had turned. It was as if *he* was now trying to kill *me*.

Our struggle may have only lasted for seconds but it felt like hours. My lungs were fit to burst. Eventually I fought him off and clawed my way to the surface.

There was a foul smell worse than singed hair when I stuck my head back out of the water. It must have been the gases that had escaped from his swollen abdomen.

Feeling somewhat sick, I headed back towards the safety of the shore. I felt relieved to think that as long as I hadn't been seen, I'd bought myself some time, maybe even gotten myself off the hook.

I hoped that if I ever had to murder again, I would make a better job of covering up my tracks and would know enough to avoid all the bungling that Brian's death had entailed.

I drove home and inspected the car. There was mud on the tyres. It could link me to the area where Brian's body had been disposed of, so I cleaned things up with a pressure washer. Then I inspected the back of the car. There was no sign of any missing eyeball or any obvious bloodstains, thank God. Still, I shuddered to think where the eyeball might be.

Perhaps unsurprisingly, given my occupation, I had second thoughts about the tyres. What if the police were able to put me at the quarry based on the tyre tracks my car had left? I'd forgotten about that. I had to change them. But it was a company car, and the company was supposed to pay for that sort of thing. If I paid for new tyres, it would attract suspicion, and the company wasn't going to pay for any new tyres until the present ones needed replacing, which they clearly did not. I needed an excuse.

I took a Stanley knife and slashed every tyre on the car. Then I rang the accounts department. I knew one of the managers there, Geoff Spencer.

"Geoff, it's Brad," I said in a grave tone of voice. "I've had some bad luck. I've had my tyres slashed by vandals and I need my car today to chase up some stories. Can you give me authorisation to get a breakdown truck to take it to the tyre depot and get some new ones right away?"

"Okay Brad, no problem. I'll make a note of it. What's the world coming to, eh?"

What indeed, I thought.

I rang up a breakdown service, got the car towed to the tyre depot, and had the tyres replaced.

The attendant behind the counter was wearing blue overalls and a bored expression. He had black greasy hair with a fringe that covered the top half of his lean garage mechanic's face.

"What happens to the old tyres when you take them off?" I asked him.

He acknowledged my presence by jerking his head to one side, swinging his floppy fringe out of his eyes.

"They get recycled. We have a collection truck coming tomorrow," he replied.

That reassured me. Tomorrow the tyres would be gone. It would be another piece of evidence consigned to history; another secret that no-one but me would ever know about.

After the tyres had been replaced, I went to a valeting service and told the staff that my car needed a thorough cleaning. I said that someone had taken a dog in it and I had an allergy to dogs, so I had to be sure that every last trace of organic matter was removed from it. They set to work and soon had it spotless. With the car cleaned up, I began to feel safer and calmed down a bit.

I went into work and told everyone I was feeling much better (which was true) and that I must have eaten something that had disagreed with me. Then I spent the rest of the day on an earth-shattering story about a man who had managed somehow to shoplift a washing machine. It was the juiciest crime story I'd had all week. It was not half as juicy as the one that I knew intimately but dared not relate to the readers of the Manchester Daily News. I very much wished that I could. As a reporter, I dearly wanted to get my teeth into a story like that. But they don't come along very often.

Being the newspaper's crime reporter, I spent a lot of my time down at the local Nick. As every journalist knows, every local Nick is a buzzing hive of leaks, innuendo, rumour, stories, and, just occasionally, the odd morsel of truth. It occurred to me that I ought to wander down there a bit more frequently in future and keep my ear close to the ground for any news of a mutilated body.

I would not have long to wait. I wasn't to know it at the time, but I hadn't been sufficiently thorough with my screwdriver work. There were coils of Brian's intestine that I'd failed to puncture. These provided a home for gases to collect in which, eventually, floated him back to the surface of the lagoon.

16

B rian's death had a devastating effect on me. Quite apart from the fear of capture that plagued me non-stop (no matter how thoroughly a villain covers up his crime, he always worries that eventually he'll get caught) I was carrying an excessively heavy burden of guilt.

Somehow I managed to handle it, although I had to slip into the toilet at frequent intervals for a good cry on my own. These outpourings of emotion made me feel better and gave me the strength to carry on.

After one such episode I felt so strong that I toyed with the idea of confronting Sandra about her relationship with Brian. But then, during the drive home, I realised I couldn't do that because it might arouse her suspicious about how he'd met with his untimely end. The details of his end had not yet come to light, but I suspected that they would not be long in doing so.

I was right.

17

There was another reason I didn't want to confront Sandra. Perhaps this was even more important than the first. Strange though it may seem, I had no desire to take her to task over her unfaithfulness. It was as if what I'd done to Brian had completely exorcised me of any desire for retribution I may have had.

Not long after I buried Brian (if you could call it a burial; I suppose it was similar to a burial at sea) I began to reconsider my life.

It became clear to me that I had to work at my relationship with Sandra. I'd let that slide for far too long and I wanted to put things right, if it wasn't too late. I could only hope she'd be willing to be open minded about me, and, more to the point, about *us*.

I'm fifty-nine years old and Sandra is thirty-five. I snatched her from the cradle some fourteen years ago, when she was only twenty-one. It caused quite a stir amongst her friends at the time. They spent a great deal of time wizz-wozzing about the fact that she was dating a man old enough to be her father (or her grandfather, as some of the wiseacres amongst them suggested).

I must admit that I'd never been entirely comfortable with the age gap between us. I didn't let on, but I often wondered what she saw in me, as many others no doubt did.

We had a good sex life at one time. We were at it like rabbits. But over the years things changed. Our sex became less frantic, more considered. Then it grew scarce, finally disappearing altogether.

I was assailed with worry about what was going on at first, but at length I resigned myself to that state of affairs. I told myself it was what happened to all relationships eventually, particularly those in which the participants were married. Occasionally, I dropped hints to Sandra that sex might be a good thing now and again, but those seeds fell (like those of my loins) on stony ground.

Having said that, the decline in our sex life was partly my own fault. Indeed, if I'm to be honest, I was more than half to blame. I don't know if it was the pressure of work and being a parent, or if it was my age, but something had happened to my sex drive since the birth of our second child, Jack. It had dramatically declined. In fact it had all but gone. I sometimes wondered whether I'd be able to do anything about it if Sandra *did* show an interest in sex. I was almost grateful that she didn't, and at the same time I was worried that she didn't.

The recognised dividing line between middle-age and old age is Sixty. That's when you're officially old. I'd found that out by consulting the Great Sage of our time, Google, and I was on the verge of it. Each day that passed brought me closer to that most significant line. It made me feel as if I was rocketing towards senility. I was looking for a brake pedal but there wasn't one.

18

"Have you heard from Brian?" Sandra asked me one day.

The expression on her face was almost the mirror image of how I felt: guilt and loss. It was suppressed of course, but obviously there, just below the surface, if you knew to look for it, as I did. She would have seen those feelings in me, had she taken any notice of my demeanour, but she was far too pre-occupied with her own feelings ever to do a thing like that.

"Brian who?" I asked with as much conviction as I could muster.

"You know, your brother Brian."

"I never hear from him. We don't get on, remember?" I snapped, with genuine annoyance.

That will stand me in good stead, I thought. *I came across as very convincing there.*

"But I thought - "

"You thought what?"

"That Brian and you - "

"That Brian and me what?"

"Nothing."

After that, Sandra never brought up the subject of my brother up again. Not until the news of his tragic end surfaced, anyway.

19

I don't know when it was exactly, but in the aftermath of Brian's death something happened in the middle of the night that hadn't happened in years. I woke up with a raging erection. It was so powerful that my penis felt as if it might be radioactive. I actually pulled up the covers and tried to see it, convinced that it must be glowing in the dark. Glowing it was not. But it was certainly red hot, like a poker in a coal fire.

It may have been that the effect of exercising power over life and death acted as an aphrodisiac on me. Whatever it was, I welcomed it.

I briefly toyed with the idea of waking up Sandra and inviting her to sate my newly found appetite, but immediately dismissed the idea. The prospects of her agreeing to sex were limited at the best of times. And three in the morning was, for Sandra, very far removed from the best of times.

By the evening of the next day I was pent up with sexual frustration. My balls were aching like never before. Once or twice during the course of the afternoon I'd considered giving myself a quick off-the-wrist job in the toilets, but it had been a busy day and a suitable opportunity had not presented itself.

My desires were so intense that I felt as if I had to restore my sex life with Sandra or seek a mistress. But of course a mistress was out of the question. It was my wife I wanted, and it wasn't just about sex. It was about love. I wanted us to have the relationship that we'd enjoyed before Brian had come between us, and before my fits of temper had driven her away from me. So I wooed her as never before, not since we'd first met, anyway, and I took nothing about her for granted.

One day after we'd packed the kids off to bed, I said to her:

"You know, I've been thinking. Things aren't the same as they used to be for us, and it's because of me. I know it is. I haven't been fair with you Sandra, not for a long time. It's poisoned our relationship. I'm trying to be better, I don't know if you've noticed. I was hoping we could make a fresh start. Do you think there's any chance of that?"

She was only half listening to me when I began talking. That had become the norm in our relationship. But as I neared the end of my little speech, I could see that she was taking it in.

"So that's what it's all been about," she said. "Doing the housework, those flowers you bought the other day, and the chocolates." (Flowers and chocolates; when I heard her saying those words, I realised what a clichéd clod I had become).

"Yes," I said sadly. "That's what it's all been about. I want us to be *us* again. Not the strange dysfunctional couple we've been for the last few years."

She shook her head. My heart sank until I realised that she wasn't rejecting my proposal.

"It's not just you," she said. "It's me. *I* haven't been fair with *you*."

I wondered if she was about to confess to her affair with Brian. I didn't need that. I didn't want it.

"It doesn't matter that you might not have been fair with me," I told her. "It was all my fault at the end of the day. It was *me* that drove *you* away."

Her face began to screw up in a familiar manner. It was what always happened just before she was going to cry. I recognised this facial expression of hers for what it was because I'd made Sandra cry many times over the years.

"It's my fault too," she said. "You don't know how much I've let you down."

This gave me the opportunity to be noble about things. I grabbed it with both hands.

"We've both let each other down but in the grand scheme of things I'm the one to blame. I'm the only one to blame. I want to get us back on track. I love you Sandra, and I hope that you feel the same way. Do you still love me? Can we get back to being the people we used to be?"

Her shoulders shook with grief, or relief, I wasn't sure which, and she threw her arms around me. She pressed her cheek to mine and her hot tears flowed down both our faces. We remained in one another's arms for several minutes. Eventually she let me go and wiped her eyes with both hands.

"You don't know how many times I've wanted to hear you talk like this," she said. "Of course I still love you, you idiot."

Being called an "idiot" was not what I'd been

aiming at, but taken in context it seemed favourable and was not the worst thing she'd ever called me.

"Does that mean you want us to be good friends again?" I asked.

She appeared to have calmed down, and possibly, even, to be pleased with our rapprochement.

"Yes of course," she said. "Let's get back to being the way we were before. Let's both make a pledge to work at it."

I didn't expect to resume sexual relations with Sandra straight away after that exchange, of course. I knew it'd be some time before we could become lovers again. But at least it seemed that if I continued to put out for her, we could get back on track, and I'd been sufficiently chastened to make that effort.

Things improved surprisingly quickly from that point on. Perhaps Brian was on Sandra's conscience as much as my own, and she wanted to make amends for what she'd done. If that was the case, then I had much to thank Brian for. Sandra and I became, if not inseparable, closer than we had ever been before.

And our sex life actually improved.

20

There was one evening when I got home before Sandra and I was absolutely gagging for it. There's no other way of putting it. My restored libido was to blame.

I did my best to get Jack and Lucy playing quietly together and then, as soon as Sandra came into the house, I pounced. She'd no sooner taken off her coat and hung it on the row of hooks in the hallway than I'd slapped her on her ample and very shapely backside.

"Get your ass upstairs," I said. "You've got some urgent work to do."

She must have been shocked. I'd never before spoken to her like that, not even when our relationship had been fresh and passionate, so I wasn't in the least surprised when she shot me a look that was meant to put me in my place in no uncertain terms.

But when her eyes met mine, the expression on her face changed. It softened, I'm not sure why. Maybe it was because she could see that I meant business; or maybe it was her way of making an effort to help us get back on track; or maybe my glands were suddenly producing the most potent pheromones in history. Whatever it was, she said:

"Brad, you seem different."

(She was right about that. I was indeed different. I was a murderer). She said it in a girly sort of way, quite giggly and rather coquettishly.

Then she said:

"What about the kids?"

"Let me worry about the kids," I told her. "You've got a serious job to do, young lady. My ball-sack is brim-full. It hasn't been emptied in months. This is an emergency."

As she went up the stairs, Sandra exaggerated the wiggle of her hips. About half way up, she turned and looked back at me over her shoulder.

"What are you waiting for?" She asked.

She hurried up the rest of the way and fell giggling into our bedroom. I followed close behind and bolted the door (I'd installed a bolt on it some years earlier to give us privacy, and now I was grateful for my foresight). I watched as she undressed.

"Don't bother taking off the bra," I told her. "And as for the knickers, I'll take them off myself. With my teeth. And you can keep the stockings and shoes on. I like it better that way."

She didn't argue. She seemed to like being told what to do. I made a mental note to do it more often.

I pulled off my t-shirt, unfastened my belt, and ripped off my boxers, then fell on Sandra like a thunderbolt. I did as I'd promised and ripped off her knickers with my teeth. Finally, I got down to the serious business at hand.

Yes, it was quick; and yes, it was dirty; but I tell

you now (and I'm not one for bragging) that we both came at the same time, and we both enjoyed it as much as either of us had ever enjoyed sex before.

"That's just for openers," I told her afterwards. "You can have the main course tonight after the kids have gone to bed."

"Have you been taking Viagra or something?" She asked.

"Of course not," I said. "Don't be silly. I'd have discussed a drastic step like that with you before I did it. You know I would. We always talk about things. You've just not given me the opportunity to show you what I can do for a long time. That's why you're surprised. You've forgotten how much energy I have."

She lay there looking stunned, like a duck that's been hit on the head.

"You've never had that much energy before," she said.

Then she kind of looked sideways at me with a big smile on her face and added:

"I'm looking forward to getting together later."

I must admit that the post-coital scenario was somewhat marred for me by the fact that I was worried about Brian.

I knew that he would soon be missed, and that at some stage there would be a concerted effort to find him. It was possible, perhaps even likely, that his body would be retrieved from the old quarry. Then there would be hell to pay if I hadn't done enough to cover up my tracks.

I wondered if I could pre-empt matters.

21

It occurred to me that if I could find a number of bodies with similar injuries to Brian's and draw these to the attention of the police, then when Brian was discovered, they might presume that whoever had killed the other victims had also killed Brian.

And that could get me off the hook.

Of course, I didn't know where there might be any bodies in a similar state to Brian's, but it seemed certain that there would be a few, more than a few, given that Jim owned equipment that had been made for the express purpose of crushing skulls and removing brains.

How could I find out where they were hidden?

The obvious place to look for information was in Jim's journal, but I'd scoured it comprehensively and had not been able to find anything that told me where the bodies were. I knew they were in some catacombs, but that was all.

There were two snags to my plan.

First, that Jim might want to claim the credit for the bodies if I found them, and if he was believed (which he surely would be) it'd be obvious that he couldn't have killed my brother. After all, he'd been behind bars when that foul deed had been done.

Second, that there could be DNA evidence on the bodies that would link them to Jim, and thereby establish that those victims were murdered by someone other than the fiend who'd killed my brother.

But I knew how to deal with those problems.

First, I'd wait for Jim to die of cancer before letting the news out. I'd seen what the medics had to say about his condition, so I knew I wouldn't have long to wait.

Second, I'd cleanse the bodies of any DNA evidence that could link them to Jim, before telling the police about them. I didn't know exactly how I was going to do that, but I reasoned there must be a way – by immersing them in a solvent of some kind, or a mild acid, or by burning them (but not to an unrecognizable crisp!).

It occurred to me that I could get Jim to reveal where the bodies were by offering him an incentive. Namely, that the bodies would help me publicise his achievements in exorcising so many troublesome demons, and thereby earn him a place in the history books.

He might refuse to tell me, of course, in which case I would explore other avenues. But he might just admit everything; it could be that simple. In any event, I had nothing to lose by asking, so I called the prison and tried to arrange a meeting with Jim. The appointments secretary sounded troubled when I asked to see him.

"I'm sorry, that's not possible." She said. "I'm afraid that Jim's condition has deteriorated badly. He's in the prison hospital and he's not well enough to receive visitors at present, not even those like you, who want to see him in an official capacity. Sorry we didn't inform you about this before."

I was stunned by the news. It was only a few weeks since I'd spoken to Jim, and even though I'd known that his death was on the cards, it shocked me to hear that he could be about to make his final exit. I always react to death in that way. I can never quite grasp the idea that someone has gone out of my life forever. I'd felt a bond with Jim during our first meeting when he'd confided in me, and that bond had grown stronger, now that we had something in common: a terrible secret. But the bond was about to be severed.

I clutched at straws.

"Did he leave any messages for anyone? For me, for instance?"

"Sorry, I can't tell you," said the secretary. "I don't know. And in any case, I can't tell you anything over the telephone because of the Data Protection Act. You'll need to come in and give me evidence of your identity if you want me to give you any information about Jim."

I thanked her for her help and said goodbye.

Although the news of Jim's illness was upsetting for me, it wasn't long before I began to look on the bright side. With him out of the way, I had greater freedom of action. It meant that if I were to find any bodies that had suffered the same fate as Brian, Jim wouldn't be around to claim the credit for them. It would be assumed that all the murders – including that of my brother – were committed by the same person.

A madman who bore no relation to me.

Now I just had to find the bodies – if, indeed, they existed. I couldn't take it for granted that all the claims made in Jim's journal were true. Not when he reckoned he was the Angel Gabriel. He might have cremated his victims, for instance. If he'd done that, I had no chance of getting the evidence I needed to prove my innocence. I could only hope that, as stated in his journal, he'd given them something akin to the decent Christian burial that I had given Brian.

There was a story I remembered working on prior to meeting Jim. I could still recall the headline:

"Manchester police now looking for fourth missing man – have you seen him?"

In the wake of this news I'd run a campaign to raise awareness about the missing men. It had lasted for several weeks and was very popular for a while. However, interest had eventually petered out, and I'd dropped the story, even though I knew of more missing men to add to the initial list of four.

I suddenly realised I had the key to the missing man story.

They were killed by Jim, I thought. *Those poor wretches probably sat in that chair in Jim's cellar and went through the most appalling agonies while he drilled holes in their skulls in the belief that he was removing Demons from them. It's just a pity he couldn't do anything about his own Demons.*

Unfortunately, my revelation brought me no closer to knowing where the bodies were.

I visited the Old Chapel and searched high and low in the garden for a hidden stairway to a set of catacombs, but found nothing. Then I performed a similar exercise in the cellar. Again, there was no secret passage or doorway leading anywhere.

I decided to ask Chu for information. He wasn't the talkative type, but I felt that if I approached him in the right way he might provide me with something I could use. Jim's journal had revealed that Chu was involved in trafficking drugs, and I wondered if I might use this information as leverage. On the other hand, I was all too aware that Drug Barons (and even their lowly serfs) are prone to react with extreme violence towards decent people like you and I, if we're seen as a threat in any way. So I knew I'd have to proceed with extreme caution.

22

C hu must have had a very good memory. When I paid my second visit to his shop, he recognised me immediately.

"You. Jim's friend. What do you want?"

His directness took me aback. I didn't want to tell him what I was after right away. I hoped to win him over first, if I could, then put my request to him, as one friend to another.

Behind him there were rows of herbal medicines stacked neatly on shelves.

"Er, I'm looking for Chinese medicine," I lied.

He seemed unconvinced.

"What kind of medicine?"

My mind worked hard to think of an illness Chu could purport to cure.

"A pick-me-up if you've got one, a sort of tonic or universal panacea. I'm feeling a bit run down."

He narrowed his eyes.

"You don't look run down."

I leant against the counter as if my legs were struggling to support me.

"I am," I insisted. "I've been under a lot of pressure lately."

That, at least, was true.

He shrugged and took a bottle from the middle shelf.

"This will re-balance your Qui. That will be £50.00 please."

Ouch.

I handed the money over. At that precise moment I must have looked genuinely ill. £50 is approximately £49 more than I would normally pay for a bottle of an over-the-counter quack remedy.

I reached into my pocket and took out a business card. It read: "Bradley Sharpe *News Reporter* Manchester Daily News." I had another version that referred to me as "Bradley Sharpe *Crime Reporter*" but felt it wouldn't be a great idea to show that one to Chu. He might not be too keen to have his crimes made public. And there were many to expose, not the least of which was his flagrant profiteering and multiple breaches of the Trades Descriptions Act.

"I just want to know about Jim. I was hoping you could tell me something about him," I said.

He put both hands on the counter and leaned towards me, a tad aggressively for my liking.

"Why are you nosing around asking me about Jim? Why don't you go to Jim and ask him what you want to know?" He demanded.

I had a good answer to that one.

"I can't. That's the whole point. Jim's dying. He was taken to the prison hospital last night. He's not likely to come out."

Chu's face fell.

"How do you know?"

I looked suitably grave.

"I called the prison this morning. They told me."

He shook his head.

"That is bad news, very bad news."

"I know. I'm sorry to be burdening you with this news. I didn't know Jim well, but he seemed like a nice chap. Anyway, the reason I want to know about him is that I'd like to write his obituary for the prison newspaper they have in Strangeways." (I didn't know if there was a "prison newspaper" that circulated around Strangeways, but it sounded convincing to me, and I thought it might convince Chu). "What can you tell me?"

I took out my notebook.

"I can't tell you anything. I didn't know anything about Jim," he said.

So I hit him with the kind of question that we investigative journalists specialize in.

"But he trusted you with the keys to his house. Surely he wouldn't have done that unless you both knew at least a little bit about each other."

There was a long silence as I shut up and studied his facial expression, just like they taught me to do at the journalists training college I'd attended in my twenties. He didn't have one. He was totally inscrutable. So I tried another tack.

"You don't have to tell me anything confidential," I said reassuringly. "Just a few snippets of information I can use to make him look good, like his hobbies and interests for instance, and his favourite places, that kind of thing."

He looked at me askance.

"It is time for you to go."

He knew how to stonewall. So did I. I glanced at my watch.

"I've got all afternoon," I told him.

His face darkened.

"No you haven't," he said. "You have ten seconds."

23

If I'd been a tough Private Detective, a Philip Marlowe type, I would have grabbed hold of Chu, dragged him across the counter, beaten some respect into him, and beaten the information I needed out of him. But violence isn't my bag. So I turned and left, in a dignified but rather hasty fashion. As I made my exit I found myself wondering if it would help Chu with his manners to have his head stuck fast in a vice for a while. I suspected that it probably would.

When I got home I pored over Jim's journals, once again trying to find something I might have missed that would lead me to a pile of bodies. My studies were interrupted by a telephone call from my mother. She sounded excited.

"Bradley," she said. "Your Dad is coming home tomorrow. Isn't that great news? He'll be arriving in the morning. Would you like to drop in to say hello to him?"

I thought about it, but not for long.

Although it was a work day and I'd have to devote a lot of it to my job, I knew I could find time to see my father. He'd just spent a week or two in hospital after suffering a serious heart attack. It was good to know he was well enough to be discharged

It was about that time that I decided to quit my voluntary work as a prison visitor. I felt I had too many commitments to give up even two hours a month of my time to visiting prisoners. For a start, I had my relationship with Sandra to think about. That was in the process of being healed, but it would require a great deal of nurturing.

Then there were my parents. They were both elderly and infirm, and were making increasing demands of me.

And as if those issues weren't enough to keep me busy, I could foresee a great deal of risk management being required in the months ahead to keep me out of the frame for Brian's murder. Part and parcel of the risk management process would entail looking for the place where Jim had hidden the bodies of his victims. God alone knew how much of my time that was going to take up.

I sent a letter to the prison authorities handing in my resignation.

I also sent a letter to Jim.

I didn't think that he would recover sufficiently to ever leave the prison hospital. He might not even recover sufficiently to read the letter. But even so, I wrote to him telling him how well I felt we'd got on, and expressing my sincere regrets that I was unable to continue to provide him with support. I wished him well for the future, even though I knew he had none, and said I hoped he wasn't too unhappy with things. Writing to him made me feel better about myself. I'd let him down by withdrawing from my role as his visitor, and my letter partly made up for it. I knew from experience that cons appreciate that sort of gesture.

The next day I visited my Mum and Dad, and was shocked to see the state Stan, my Dad, was in. He could speak but his speech was slow and slurred; his right arm trembled, and he walked with a limp. He seemed weak and feeble. It made me feel like crying.

Inwardly, although I didn't say anything to my parents, I blamed Brian for Dad's condition. He was always getting into arguments with Dad, and stressing him out. I pictured my brother bobbing about in the dark lagoon. *Serves him right,* I thought.

As soon as I got the opportunity, I cornered my mother in the kitchen where my dad couldn't hear us talk.

"What did they say about him when he was discharged?" I asked in a low voice. "Did they mention anything about him improving?"

"Yes, love," she told me. "They told me he might get better or he might not. No-one seemed to know for sure." Tears began to roll down her cheeks. "They said that if he did improve, it could take months."

I felt tears welling up myself, but I held them in. I had to be strong for my parents.

"Oh my God," I said, giving her a hug. "I'm so sorry. I'd expected he'd be back to his old self."

My Dad was ordinarily an old curmudgeon, but now he seemed too feeble even to enjoy being miserable and making others miserable. Strange though it seemed, I was missing that quality.

I returned to the front room. He was sitting in his favourite armchair with a tartan blanket across his lap. My mother had wanted to throw the armchair out decades ago, but he hadn't let her. It was threadbare and soiled with age. My dad got a kick out of the fact that the rest of us were revolted by it.

"Dad," I said. "How are you feeling now?"

He slowly looked up at me. The expression on his face never changed.

"Well, not too bad, you know," he replied in a quiet voice.

I took Chu's medicine out of my pocket.

"I've got something here that might help you. It's a Chinese medicine. It's said to be very potent. Would you like to try it?"

I don't know what made me do that. I suppose I was willing to try anything that might make my Dad well, even Chinese quackery.

"All right then. If you think it's a good idea."

I went into the kitchen, took the stopper off the medicine bottle and poured some of the liquid it contained into a glass. It was a cloudy green colour. When I took it into the room, my dad looked at it doubtfully. In spite of that, when I held it to his lips, he took a sip. After he'd tasted it, he took the glass from me with a trembling hand and gulped the rest down.

"That tasted nice."

"I'm not convinced it'll do any good Dad," I said. "But we can hope."

"It's a funny thing Brad," he replied. "I've got a good feeling about that medicine you've given me. Where did you get it?"

"From a Chinese herbalist called Chu."

"Well, we'll see."

It may have been coincidence, but my Dad's condition steadily improved from then on.

Perhaps there is a God who looks on me in a kindly way from time to time. It is to be hoped.

Now, more than ever, it is to be very much hoped.

24

Because I hadn't had a visit from the police, or heard anything on the grapevine about a body, I was beginning to feel rather good about things. So good that I allowed myself to entertain the notion that I might have got away scot-free.

Then I received a telephone call from my mother.

"Brad, have you heard anything about our Brian?" She asked.

It was an innocent question, but under the circumstances it felt like a rusting knife being twisted in my intestines.

"No," I said, straining to remain calm, "should I have?"

"Not really," she replied. "It's just that I haven't been able to get in touch with him at home, and he isn't answering his mobile. When I rang his work they said they hadn't seen him or heard from him in a while."

Naturally, I did my best to reassure her.

"I'm sure it's nothing. He's probably taken a holiday and forgotten to book the time off work. You know how absent-minded he can be."

"I don't think it's anything like that," she replied. "I'm worried he's had an accident. Do you think you could call the hospitals and check?"

"All right mother. If it'll make you feel any better, I'll do that."

I rang around and discovered that no hospital in the region had a patient by the name of Brian Sharpe. I could have saved myself the trouble, as I knew in advance what the result would be, but I thought that if there was some sort of investigation of my activities in the future, it might help if there was evidence of brotherly concern.

After I'd found out what I already knew, I called my mother back.

"I've checked all the hospitals in the region, Mum," I told her. "Brian isn't in any of them. But that's probably a good thing."

"Please come over. I've got a spare key for Brian's apartment. I'd like you to take it and go there to see if there's any indication of where he might be."

I didn't want to undertake that task, as it would involve me in the same waste of time that ringing up the hospitals had done, and there was only so much brotherly concern that I was capable of showing.

"I don't think he'd like me to do that, Mum," I said. "I'm concerned for his safety, just like you, but as you know, me and Brian don't get on too well. He'll go ape shit if he finds out I've been snooping in his apartment without his permission."

"Please, Brad, do it for me. I'll tell him I put you up to it. I've got a bad feeling about this. I feel we need to find our Brian before it's too late."

It was already too late, but I couldn't tell her that, so I relented.

"All right, Mum. If it'll help you feel any better, I'll do it. Just remember though, you've got to square it with Brian if he kicks off about it. I'll be right over."

The next day I heard rumours about the discovery of a badly mutilated body.

25

Apparently even hardened policemen were shocked by the state it was in. They'd never seen anything like it before. I visited the Nick and met up with Bob Napper, my contact there.

Bob is what you'd call a copper's copper: big, overweight, and constantly talking of retirement with a wistful expression on his fat red face.

He told me about the body in hushed tones, as if it would be sacrilegious to discuss it out loud.

"It's down in the old quarry," he said, shaking his head in disbelief at what he'd heard, "the one on the road out to Alderley. A bloke walking his dog discovered it this morning. I haven't seen it myself, but I've been told it looks like it might be some sort of ritualistic killing. There's a hole the size of your fist been drilled in the top of his head. And that's the least of what's been done to him."

I felt that Bob was exaggerating the size of the hole, but I let it go.

"What do you mean by ritualistic? Black Magic or something?" I asked, in as naïve a fashion as I could manage.

"It's too early to tell, but it could be," he said. "Or it could be the sort of sick ritual that some serial killers use."

I could see the makings of a good story in what he had just told me. Two good stories.

"You said there's a hole on top of his head, but you implied there might be other injuries. What are they?"

I felt I had to ask, even though I was probably more familiar with them than the forensic team that'd been assigned to investigate the crime scene.

He lowered his head and shook it again.

"His skull has been crushed by some sort of mechanism, possibly a vice. One of his eyeballs has been removed. We're still searching for that. Someone tried to gut him like a fish. And it looks as if every bone in his body has been broken. We're not sure yet how much of this was done while he was still alive. Maybe all of it. I'll let you know."

I made a sort of whistling sound, as if drawing in my breath at the savagery of it.

"The poor Devil," I said. "Have you any leads to go on, as to who might have done it?"

"It's too early to say. We'll be knocking on doors and putting out a request for witnesses within the next few hours. We're still waiting for forensics to finish their examination of the crime scene. They might come up with something."

I shuddered inwardly at the thought of what forensics might find.

"When can I write up the story?"

"Wait until later. I'll have a bit more for you by then."

In some ways I began to look forward to my next

briefing from Bob. It would give me the opportunity to ask as many questions of the police as I wanted about their investigations into my affairs. And it would allow me to devote a delicious hour or two to writing up the story of my exploits in suitably lurid prose.

A few hours later, Bob called with more details about the victim, an unidentified white male six foot one in height with lank brown hair (what was left of it), a circular-shaped opening cut into the top of his head, a missing eye, and a crushed skull; and other injuries consistent with every major joint in his body having been pulverised with a blunt instrument.

It was too early to identify the victim, but the usual checks were being made.

26

My first column about the murder informed readers that the identity of the victim was unknown (at least to the Greater Manchester Police) and that the cause of death had yet to be established (although, I reflected, the gaping hole in his skull offered some clue). It put forward the novel theory that the killing could have been ritualistic in some way, and it cleverly linked the ritual idea to Black Magic, a subject which is always good for the sale of a few thousand extra copies of any provincial newspaper.

I added, for good measure, that the concrete slippers (I didn't actually use this expression) could indicate a gangland hit, and that the other injuries might have been the result of torture during the course of the hit.

The press, at this stage, weren't allowed near the area where the body had been discovered, so I dug up some old stock photos of the quarry and dreamt up some interesting captions for them ("the path from which the man walking his dog first noticed a strange object floating in the water"; "the sinister lagoon in which the mutilated body of the victim was discovered"; "The sheer drop from which the victim may have been thrown to his death" etc.)

It seemed to go down rather well. At any rate, the editor liked it and the circulation was considerably up for the day.

It wasn't just the MDN that reported on the murder; many other newspapers did, and it even made the six o'clock news on the BBC. But the MDN was there first, and had (by common consent) the best coverage. As you can imagine, with so many journalists in on the act, the story was covered from every conceivable angle. Even so, one aspect of the murder that all the reports, including my own, failed to cotton onto was the fact that the murderer was an inept bungler who knew nothing at all about how to dispose of a body.

On reflection, I was pleased that this was so. Had the murderer shown more expertise when it came to concealing the evidence of his deed, I would have had nothing to report, and my career would have remained in the doldrums.

Writing about the "Skull Crusher" (the name that my column gave to Manchester's latest major criminal) gave me a buzz about myself and my job for the first time in years.

While I was working on the story, Kimberley Jones, an attractive young reporter new to the MDN (she had only a few weeks previously been working for the Lancashire Post), asked me what it was about. When I told her, she was greatly impressed - once she'd gotten over her initial feelings of nausea.

"Is that the most interesting story you've ever done?" She asked.

I was flattered by her attentions. Having a woman express any interest in me or in my activities was something that hadn't happened to me in a long time. I'd forgotten how good it felt.

"In some ways, yes," I replied. "It's a story with enough blood and gore to satisfy the most ardent murder fan. And it has an element of mystery: why would anyone kill and mutilate another person in such a vicious way? Why not just, well, kill your victim? There are so many angles to it. But in terms of pure intrigue, I'm not sure it's the *best* story I've ever worked on."

She leaned so close to me that her breasts for a moment brushed against my arm. I tried not to look too pleased about it.

"What was your *best ever* story?" She asked.

I didn't have to think very hard about what it had been.

"It was the theft of the Holy Water from the Church of St Barnabas," I replied.

She looked gratifyingly amazed.

"What? What's that again?" She asked.

"You heard me right," I told her. "The theft of the Holy Water from the Church of St Barnabas. Now, strictly speaking, it wasn't theft, because the Holy Water is made available for parishioners to use free of charge. They don't have to pay for it. But there was a period when all the stocks of holy water were being taken by someone, a particular individual, on a regular basis. He seemed to know when the priest had put the Holy Water out, then would bide his time until the priest disappeared and pounce. He'd take the lot, before any of the parishioners could get their hands on it. He didn't do it all the time. It would happen every day for a week or so, then stop. Months later, it'd happen again. Word of it got out to me, and I did a little story about it."

She was wide-eyed but had a knowing allure with it.

"That's weird. And fascinating. I'd like to move into crime reporting myself. It makes my work seem dull."

Kimberley wrote the weekly pull-out women's supplement for the MDN, and covered the goings-on in various community groups.

I hadn't taken much notice of her prior to our conversation. Probably because I'd been off sex for a long time, and hadn't been looking at women in the way I used to when I had my Mojo. But since Brian's death my Mojo had come back with a vengeance and I noticed her all right. She had high cheekbones, hair that was immaculately styled in a black bob, flashing blue eyes, and a full mouth emphasised by an artful slash of red lipstick. She had great legs that she crossed and uncrossed. A lot. Had I been her manager, it was behaviour I would have done much to encourage.

"I'm sure you'll get your chance to make a sideways move if you want to," I told her. "You just have to set your stall out right. You could come with me to a crime scene sometime to see what's involved, if you want."

I half expected her to demur. I saw myself as an old bore that no one wanted to associate with.

"That would be nice," she replied, crossing her legs for about the tenth time in as many seconds. I fought hard to keep my eyes on her face. It was a battle I was losing. She didn't seem to mind.

"I'll let you know when something comes up that's suitable for us to look at together," I said.

I'm not sure whether I said it to her face or to her legs, but she seemed suitably grateful.

"Thanks Brad, that's very good of you," she replied. "Please do. I'm looking forward to it."

The area where the reporters do their jobs at the MDN is a large open plan office covering an entire floor of News Towers (the MDN HQ on Deansgate). Kimberly's desk was across the room from mine, twenty yards away from me. After we'd had that conversation I got into the habit of raising my head from my work and looking at her, and more often than not I'd find that she was staring at me. Funny, even though the human pupil is only the size of the head of a drawing pin, I could tell she was focused on me. Her eyes would meet mine, and she'd quickly look down at her desk. Or sometimes I'd smile, and she'd give me a demure smile back, before looking away.

So I began to think the unthinkable: that I had suddenly become attractive to Kimberley Jones. This was something that would have been impossible only a short while before.

Prior to Brian's death, I'd developed an old man's negative outlook on life and had walked around with my head down, and my shoulders slumped.

Things had changed after I'd hastened Brian's departure from this mortal coil. I felt as if I'd taken control of my life, and was no longer a loser. I began to hold myself differently, and to walk differently. I held my head high, my shoulders back, and I looked people straight in the eye.

Perhaps the new me was capable of being attractive to women for the first time in years. One thing was for sure: the new me had a sex drive for the first time in years.

That was a very positive development.

But there was also a very big negative development looming over my life.

In the middle of the night, after I'd written that first story about the murder, I woke up in a state of panic.

I realised that it would be only a matter of time before Brian was identified as the victim and that when the news came out, Jed Barker, the private detective, would put two and two together. He'd realise that I'd had a motive for murdering Brian, and he'd go to the police with the photographs of Brian and Sandra. I would be pulled in for questioning, investigated thoroughly, and the game would be up.

Pools of sweat gathered in the palms of my hands as I contemplated being exposed.

The terrifying thought hit me that I could be incarcerated forever, or at least, to the end of my life, which amounted to the same thing. I didn't know it at the time, but there are worse fates than incarceration.

I had to do something about Jed Barker, but what?

It was obvious what.

I flinched from it, but I knew deep down that there was only one course of action open to me to silence Jed.

And I spent the rest of the night lying awake in bed, wondering how and when I could get him to take a dose of a sedative strong enough to enable me to load him onto a sack-cart.

27

The following morning I sprang out of bed like a man possessed. There wasn't a moment to lose. The police would identify Brian at any minute, the news about the identity of the victim would reach Jed, and he would finger me to the authorities.

As I hastily washed and dressed, I hatched schemes for doing away with him. It wouldn't be straightforward; he was nobody's fool. It would require a convincing excuse to meet with him. And as we were not in the habit of meeting for drinks, administering a sedative could prove tricky. I had no idea how I was going to go about it. I needed to somehow get him into a private situation where it would be natural for me to offer him refreshments.

Luckily it was Sandra's turn to deal with the kids that morning, so I was able to make an early exit to work and get on with formulating my plan. As I sat at my desk pretending to be working, my mind raced with the possibilities.

The plan I came up with was at best makeshift. It had to be. There was insufficient time to conceive of a masterstroke, and anyway, I was stressed out and it was difficult to think clearly. It's funny how the prospect of life imprisonment can knock you out of your stride.

At length I telephoned Jed.

"I need your help again," I said. "Can I come over?"

"What is it Brad?" He asked.

He sounded suspicious as he always did. That must be what happens to you when you make your living by prying into other people's dirty business.

"It's private. I'd rather not say on the telephone."

"Okay, come over. I'll be in all morning."

I parked in the vicinity of the building where his office was located. It was a low-rent high-rise place in the Northern Quarter. I made my way to the top floor (which must have been the cheapest) and pressed the button next to his door. He buzzed me in.

Jed had one room, one window, one desk, one filing cabinet, and one cupboard. The only things he had two of were chairs. I deposited my butt in the spare one.

"I'm worried, Jed. It's about Brian. You know those photos you took? I showed them to him. We had a massive row about it. Afterwards he was very apologetic and he got depressed. He's never been very stable. He's got what you might call a brittle personality. Anyway, he's disappeared. No-one seems to know where he is. I'm worried that he might be planning on doing something...you know... something stupid."

Jed looked perplexed.

"Like taking his own life?" He asked.

I struck up an expression of brotherly concern.

"Yes, like taking his own life."

He took off his glasses, wiped them, and put them back on again.

"I'm not sure I can help with that sort of thing. It sounds like you might need a psychiatrist."

I contorted my features into something resembling worry. It wasn't that difficult; I had a great deal preying on my mind.

"You don't understand. I need you to find him before it's too late. You do missing person stuff. If anyone can find him, you can, Jed. I'm sure you've got a lot on, but do you think you can help me, this morning if at all possible? I've got a terrible feeling about it. I think we need to act fast."

The only way we could have acted fast enough was by getting into a time machine and going back to the week before last. But anyway, I must have looked suitably concerned to Jed. That's because I *was* concerned. It was just that it was the safety of my own hide that concerned me, not Brian's.

I was sure Jed wouldn't let me down. I'd been giving him work from the Manchester Daily News for at least two decades. At times the MDN work had been all he had coming in, so he knew he had to keep me sweet. He'd done that in the past by buying me bottles of spirits at Christmas, and other presents on birthdays and so on. He had even, on one occasion, pushed the boat out and paid for an expensive family holiday for me, Sandra, and the kids. But his account was still in debit as far as I was concerned, and he knew it. He looked at his watch.

"All right, Brad," he said. "I'm very busy, but I can make a start. I can give it till lunchtime, and then I'll have to fit it in when I can during the week. What can you tell me about your brother?"

I told him what little I knew about Brian's friends and activities, then played my trump card.

"Listen, Jed, I've got a key to Brian's apartment. It's only twenty minutes away. Do you think you could come with me and take a look at the place? See if there's anything there that could explain where he is? I'd do it myself, but I'd like an expert to cast his eye over it."

I could see what Jed was thinking: *in for a penny, in for a pound.*

"All right Brad. I've just about got time, and you never know what we might find there," he said. "There's probably an innocent explanation for your brother's disappearance and we could just find it in his flat. It's worth looking."

He stood up, put on his white trench coat, and a grey trilby with a black hatband. He looked almost like a cartoonist's version of what a gumshoe should look like. Anyway, I was glad he was wearing a hat; it might make it difficult to identify him if the security cameras picked him up. I donned my own headgear, a flat cap (they had recently become fashionable) purchased on the way to Jed's office, especially for use that day.

He opened his only cupboard, pressed some buttons on a keypad, and a burglar alarm started bleeping.

"We have thirty seconds to get out of here," he said, ushering me towards the door.

Damn, I thought, *I didn't know he had an alarm. This is going to complicate matters.*

We descended the back stairs and emerged in the car park at the rear of the building.

"We'll have to take your car," I told him. "Mine's in the garage."

He gave me a narrow-eyed, sideways sort of look.

"How did you get here?" He asked.

"I had to take a taxi," I replied.

That seemed to satisfy him.

We both got in his car and he drove us to Brian's apartment block.

"You might want to park round the corner," I said, mindful of the security cameras. "The car park at the apartments is likely to be full."

He raised his eyebrows.

"No it isn't. I did the surveillance job here, don't you remember? I know what this place is like," he snapped.

For him to be that tetchy, I must have dragged him away from some very high-paying work for a premium client.

"Sorry, I don't go to Brian's apartment very often," I explained. "I didn't know that."

We turned into the car park. I looked up cautiously from under the neb of my flat cap and saw at least one security camera watching us.

Like any criminal, I calculated the risk.

We were both wearing headgear that would conceal our faces from the cameras. That gave me deniability. For all anyone knew, two unknown males had used Jed's car to visit the apartment block where Brian lived; or Jed had visited my brother's apartment block with an unidentifiable companion in tow.

It was one of the chic new developments built towards the end of the housing boom. It should have been out of Brian's financial reach, but the developer had built it with people like him in mind. A large number of the apartments were about the size of the average rabbit hutch. Granted, they cost a lot more than a rabbit hutch, but rather less than apartments of a reasonable (i.e., habitable) size. This made them affordable to the likes of my brother.

We took the lift to Brian's Rat Box on the fifth floor and let ourselves in.

Jed began poking about, inspecting all the loose bits of paper that were lying around the place.

"I'll look at the computer when I've gone through the paperwork," he told me. "I may have to take it away with me."

I nodded, trying my best to look as if I gave a damn about what he looked at.

The apartment consisted of a small living room with kitchen units down one side of it, a smaller bedroom, and a tiny shower room. There were books everywhere, mainly fiction, and a few pictures of literary figures on the walls. I went into the bedroom and found the likely location of the hidden camera that Jed had installed to take the compromising pictures of Brian and Sandra. Seeing Brian's unmade bed made me momentarily feel sick at the recollection of what had gone on in it, especially when I noticed dark stains on the valance sheet.

I returned to the front room and put the kettle on.

"I'm making a cup of tea, do you want one?" I asked as innocently as I could.

"No thanks," Jed replied. "I had one just before you came to my office."

My heart sank.

How was I to administer the sedative? Once again, I was faced with the fact that normal people can't do criminal acts for love or money. I wondered what a real criminal in my position might do. Then I thought of something. There was a small sculpture on Brian's bedside table. It appeared to be a replica of some classical statue or other. It was about a foot high. I returned to the bedroom and picked it up.

It was solid and rather heavy.

That would be my sedative.

28

I took the statue to the bathroom and wrapped it in one of Brian's smelly old towels. I didn't want to split Jed's head open. Copious quantities of blood were to be avoided.

For the time being, anyway.

When I returned to the living room, Jed was still examining scraps of paper. I reckoned he'd be feeling frustrated, as all he would find on them were half-finished remnants of the half-baked tales Brian referred to, rather ambitiously to my mind, as "short stories".

He was standing with his back to me, head down, with a number of papers in his hands. He must have found them puzzling, covered, as they were, in handwritten lines of non-rhyming nonsense. At any rate, he didn't seem to be making progress with his investigation. It occurred to me that he might be forgiven for concluding that the stories indicated that my brother had disappeared completely up his own backside.

I strode up to him quietly but purposefully with the statue in my right hand, raised high, ready to deal him a blow that would put out his lights for a good long while.

As I approached Jed, I wondered how the Manchester Daily News would report the matter of his demise. I even composed a few random statements about him that might make it into his obituary. ("Fearless investigator who shone a bright light into the murky gloom of the Manchester Underworld"; "man of unimpeachable integrity who refused to be bought"; "Jed Barker was known for adhering to the highest standards in both his professional and his personal life.").

For an instant I held the statue over his head to strike.

Then I hesitated.

I couldn't do it.

I'd thought after I'd killed Brian I had crossed my Rubicon and was capable of anything, but apparently I hadn't, and I wasn't. I didn't hate Jed; I was worried about what he might do. Somehow that wasn't sufficient motive for me to take him permanently out of the picture. I retreated to the bedroom and put the statue back in its place.

"Nothing here," Jed said eventually. "I want to spend some time with that computer of his. I'm going to disconnect it and take it with me."

He put the computer in the back of his car, little knowing how close he had come to mysteriously disappearing, just like my brother had done. He gave me a lift back to News Towers. From there I had to take a taxi to recover my car, as I'd parked it in the vicinity of Jed's office.

It must have been one of the most bodged murder attempts in history. As bodges go, it wasn't as bad as my attempts to conceal Brian's body, but it was embarrassing.

The police investigation into the death of the unidentified male moved swiftly into high gear, perhaps owing to the severity of the crime.

It wasn't long before I received a very significant official phone call. It came while I was at work.

"Brad," said the receptionist, "It's someone from the police for you."

I nearly fainted from shock just at the mention of those words: *It's someone from the police for you.* Anyway, I did my best to sound calm and relaxed.

"Please put them through."

"Mr. Sharpe," said the voice at the other end.

"Speaking," I replied.

"I'm Sydney Braithwaite from the Manchester Constabulary Special Ops department. I have something to ask you."

Apprehension clawed at my intestines.

"Fire away, Mr Braithwaite," I said.

My voice sounded strangely strangled to my own ears. I wondered what it must have sounded like to the cop at the other end of the line.

"I'd like you to help me with an investigation. In an ideal world I'd be asking you in person, but this is an urgent matter and I have to get you involved as quickly as possible."

I decided that the best policy would be to present myself as the very model of a co-operative citizen.

"I'll help in any way I can, Mr Braithwaite. Just tell me what it is that you want."

"Please call me Syd. This is a very difficult matter, Mr Sharpe. Like I said, I'd rather ask you in person, but circumstances oblige me to broach this difficult matter with you over the phone. You know of course about the body that was discovered in the old quarry?"

"Yes I do. Please call me Brad."

"Thank you, Brad. I'm sorry to have to tell you this, but we have reason to believe that the body may be the body of your brother. I'd like you to meet with me at the morgue to identify it, if you're willing to do that."

I wondered how to react. With grief or with horror? After some deliberation, I decided on mild shock and a modicum of disbelief.

"My God. Can it really be our Brian? Of course I'm willing to go to the morgue and look at the body. I can only hope that you're wrong."

"Thank you, Brad. Can you come right away?"

"I'll set off immediately."

We ended the conversation and I headed for the morgue wondering what lay in store for me there.

Syd was waiting by the entrance. He was about six foot two, middle-aged, and red haired with grey flecks at his temples. Beneath his chin was a succession of smaller chins, like offspring of the original. They wobbled as he spoke.

"Brad?" He asked as I approached.

"That's right. Are you Syd?"

"Yes. Before we go in, I need to warn you about what you're going to see. It may be rather upsetting for you. The victim was put through a terrible ordeal before his death, and afterwards the body was left to decompose. You need to be prepared for what he looks like. I hope you have a strong constitution. I'd like you to stay long enough to identify the body one way or another for us, if you possibly can. But if you find the experience too upsetting, please feel free to leave at any time."

I manipulated my features into an expression of the utmost gravity mingled with a steely determination, and just a hint of anxiety.

"I'll do my best Syd," I assured him.

We entered the building and headed for the cold room.

"You better put this on," he said, handing me a respirator as we approached the final door.

He put one on himself.

Then we went in and I saw the thing lying on a cold slab.

The thing that Brian had become.

It was covered by a white sheet. When Syd pulled the sheet back, I saw it was blue-green in colour, and I could tell just by the look of it that it stank to high heaven. I was grateful for the respirator.

Even though I was the one who'd done that to Brian and should have known what to expect, I was shocked by what I saw. More than shocked, I was disgusted and appalled.

The ghastly thing lying there didn't even resemble my brother. For an instant I thought they were showing me someone else, possibly one of Jim's victims. But then I looked more closely and recognised the sneering curl of its mouth. That was him all right. But I didn't say so too quickly; it might have looked suspicious for me to easily identify the thing lying on the slab as my brother, when it barely even looked human. So I looked here and there at the head from different angles, as if making sure it was Brian, before finally I nodded and said:

"Yes, it's him," while maintaining on my face a suitable expression of gravity.

I didn't waste any time trying to look as if I was on the verge of tears or anything like that.

"I'm sorry, Brad," said Syd. "I can't imagine how it feels."

Quite good in some ways, actually, I thought. *If only I knew for sure that I could get away with it.*

Syd and I left the morgue and I asked him if he'd inform my parents. I told him that I wasn't sure I had the heart to tell them myself.

"It's all right, Brad, I'll do it," he said. "It's standard police procedure in these situations, and I know how hard it must be for you. You've never done anything like this before, and it's a member of your own family. I've had plenty of experience at this sort of thing, and I wasn't related to Brian. Even so, I have to say, it's the worst job in the force. Everybody hates it."

Outside in the daylight he gave me an earnest jutting-jaw policeman look.

"We'll do everything we can to catch the person who did this to your brother, Brad," he assured me. "Everything. Don't you worry about that."

That's exactly what I am worried about, I thought.

29

O n my return to the office I wrote a powerful
follow-up to my first story about the murder.

I informed my readers that the victim had been
identified as a local man, Brian Sharpe, and I again
referred to the perpetrator as the "Skull Crusher".

The quarry where Brian had been found was no
longer off-limits, so I went there with a photographer
to take pictures to illustrate my story. A picture paints
a thousand words, after all.

Having been briefed by the police, I could safely
include information in my column that I'd been
obliged to keep out of my first account of the murder.
For instance, I was able to confirm that the body had
indeed been thrown down the sheer rock face. (This
had been no more than speculation before) and, to
bring the point to life, I included a photograph of the
rock face with a line of black dashes superimposed
over it, dramatically indicating the likely trajectory
the body might have taken while in flight.

I also included a picture of the lagoon with a
black arrow helpfully pointing to the wooden

platform that had "brought the descent of the victim to a sudden and most painful halt." (The police hadn't yet released the information that the victim had died before he'd even begun his journey to the quarry, nor had they mentioned the puncture marks in his abdomen caused by my slot-Head screwdriver).

The murder was far more fulfilling for me to write about than the usual fare that came my way. Dreary stories about drink-driving, car theft, and petty vandalism. (Jeremy Sykes of Didsbury was found guilty of urinating in a shop doorway late last Friday night. He was fined £50.00 and bound over to keep the peace for three months.").

I like to think I'm an optimist, but some of this stuff depressed even me. I wanted my criminals to provide me with better stories than this; stories I could wax lyrical about. And at last, one of them had stepped up to the plate and delivered. The fact that he happened to be me did not detract one iota from the enthusiasm with which I reported his exploits. Indeed, if anything, it added to it.

Shortly after I finished typing up the story, I received a call from Peter Saxon, the Editor.

"Brad," he said. "Do you think you could come to my office please?"

"Sure," I told him. "When would you like to see me?"

"Right away if possible."

"I'm on my way."

I strolled to the corner of News Towers where Peter's office was located and went in. He looked up from his desk.

"Take a seat Brad."

He was looking distinctly humourless, which was unusual for him.

"What's this about Pete?" I asked. "Is there a problem?"

"Not exactly. I've been looking at this story of yours. The one about the Skull Crusher. The victim was called Brian Sharpe. One of our secretaries told me that your brother is called Brian Sharpe. I don't like to ask this, Brad, but I have to. Was the victim your brother by any chance?"

I allowed myself to appear upset, but in control.

"I'm afraid he was, Pete."

"That must be awful for you. God alone knows what you're going through. You should have told me. There was no need for you to come in and write up that story, of all stories. I'd have given you compassionate leave right away. You must take some time off to come to terms with your loss. I'll authorise an extended period of leave on full pay for you."

He couldn't have known it, but that was the very last thing I wanted. If he put me on leave, I'd have no excuse to go snooping down at the Nick for news about the progress of the investigation into my late brother's death. And that was a subject dear to my heart.

"That's very kind of you Pete, but I can't accept your offer," I told him.

He looked stunned. Every other employee on the MDN payroll would have jumped at the chance of having an extended period of leave on full pay.

"Why not?" He asked.

"I don't want to be left alone with my thoughts Pete," I explained. "I know I'll feel much better if I have something to do. The days ahead will be long and painful if I have to spend them on my own, contemplating my brother's, well, you know, contemplating what's happened."

"I understand. I think I'd feel the same way in your shoes. But just remember, you can always change your mind. That offer stays open. Take advantage of it, if you need to. Don't be shy about it."

I looked suitably grateful.

"Thanks Pete. It's reassuring to know."

"Oh, and another thing. You don't have to work on any more stories involving your late brother. Just give me the word and I'll pass them on to someone else."

"There's no need for that, Pete. I actually want to write all the stories I can about this. It'll make me feel as if I'm doing something to help Brian. If I can raise public awareness about his death, a witness might come forward. It could help to catch his killer. And one thing I'd love to do right now is help catch the perp."

"Okay Brad, if that's what you want to do, you've got my full support. I'll let you have as much coverage as you want for your brother, provided it can somehow be justified within the editorial policy of the newspaper. I'll bend the rules as much as I can to accommodate you."

I looked even more grateful than before. That's because my gratitude was genuine. Saxon's offer meant I'd be able to monitor any developments in the hunt for Brian's killer, and it would all be in the guise of helping the police to catch him.

"Thanks Pete. I'll get back to work now."

I returned to my desk feeling better about things, but I still had concerns. In particular, I was worried about the flak I'd have to deal with when Jed went to the police with his revelations about Brian's affair with my wife.

30

I tried not to dwell on that prospect. I told myself it'd work out all right in the end. But I must admit that every time I wasn't otherwise occupied, I was mentally rehearsing answers to every line of police questioning I could think of. And whenever I did that, I got butterflies in my stomach.

That evening as soon as Sandra got home, I went into the kitchen with her, making sure we were out of earshot of the kids.

"Please sit down, Sandra," I said. "I've got something to tell you."

She looked troubled. Perhaps she was worried I was going to bring up the subject of her affair with Brian. She pulled a chair out from under the table and apprehensively sat on it. I took a seat myself.

"It's about Brian," I said. She went from troubled to panic stricken. "There's no easy way to tell you this. He's dead."

Her expression changed from panic to an odd combination of sadness and relief. I think it was mostly relief.

"Dead?" She repeated. "But how?"

"In the worst way imaginable," I told her. "You know that killer I've been writing about? The "Skull Crusher"? Well, there's no way I can dress this up, I'm afraid, the man who was found in the quarry, with his skull crushed, was our Brian."

She put her hands to her face and began to sob.

"I'm sorry. You must think it's ridiculous of me to get so upset when I didn't even know Brian that well."

"No," I reassured her. "I don't think it's at all ridiculous. I know what a caring person you are. I knew this would affect you. Shall I make us both a cup of tea?"

She shook her head; she couldn't speak. I put the kettle on. I wasn't going to let my own grief stop me from enjoying a cup of tea.

While I sat at the table sipping my tea, Sandra did her best to pull herself together.

"I suppose we'll have to tell the children," she said at last.

Her face was puffy and red from crying.

"That's right," I agreed. "The sooner the better, really. We want them to hear this from us first, not from their friends."

We got the kids together in the front room.

"Has Mummy been crying?" Lucy asked.

"Yes," I said, "Mummy is very upset about something. You two will have to be nice to her and cheer her up."

Jack and Lucy immediately ran to Sandra and each of them took a leg and hugged it.

"I've got some grown-up news for you both," I told them. They liked anything grown-up. "But I'm afraid it's bad news."

Jack looked perplexed.

"What is it?" Lucy asked.

"It's about Uncle Brian," I said. That was sufficient to lose Jack's interest. He hadn't met Uncle Brian very often and when he had, Uncle Brian had shown a startling ineptitude for interacting with children. "I'm afraid he's died, Lucy."

She looked puzzled.

"Does that mean we won't see him again?" She asked.

"I'm afraid it does."

"Can I go and play with my friends now?" She asked.

"Yes of course."

She scampered out of the room and Jack quickly followed. Their heavy footsteps woke up Jenny the family cat. She raised her head and watched them leave with a pissed off expression on her face, then she settled her head back on the rug for another good long kip.

"That went rather well," I said to Sandra.

She fled from the room and I heard her sobbing quietly in the kitchen.

Then my mobile rang.

"Is that Brad Sharpe?"

"Yes. How can I help?"

"It's Syd here, Syd Braithwaite. We met this afternoon. I'm outside your parents' house. I've just seen them to tell them about your brother. They haven't taken the news at all well, which is understandable, of course. I think you better get over here and spend some time with them."

My heart sank. I couldn't imagine what they must have been going through.

"Thanks Syd," I said. "I'll be right over."

31

I went to the kitchen where Sandra was sitting at the table looking forlorn. I had a degree of sympathy for her, more than a degree. I could imagine how distressing it was for her to have lost her lover, and to have lost him in such a sickening way. She'd be wondering what sort of suffering he'd been subjected to before he'd breathed his last. And she couldn't discuss her feelings with me, because her feelings for Brian were something that could never be aired, not in my presence, anyway. So she'd just have to bottle those feelings up. I knew how painful that could be.

It could eat away at you for years if you let it.

I crouched and put my arm around her shoulders.

"Sandra, I'm sorry, I have to go. I know you're upset, and I don't want to leave you, but the police have just told my parents about Brian. I'm going to have to get over there. They're in bits. I won't be too long, I promise."

"That's all right. Take your time, Brad. They need you even more than I do right now. I know that."

She was being a brave soldier for me. I appreciated her sacrifice.

"Thanks love," I said. "I'll be back as soon as I can."

I let myself in to my Mum and Dad's house without knocking. That was accepted practice in our family. I think it's a working class thing.

As soon as I got inside I heard my mother crying her heart out, and when I entered the front room, she looked up at me over the top of a handkerchief she was holding to her face. My father was just looking glum. It was difficult to tell how upset he might have been, because glum was his default expression.

"Brad," sobbed my mother, "thank God you're here."

She got out of her chair and ran up to me, and we hugged for a minute or two without speaking. My Dad was still faring poorly from his heart attack, but he made the effort to stand up and come over to me. He just sort of stood next to me, and both of us felt uncomfortable. The truth is, neither of us knew what to do. My dad and I didn't have the sort of relationship where we hugged each other. In his day, blokes didn't do that kind of thing.

"I'll make us all a cup of tea," I said.

I seemed to be saying that a lot lately.

I made three mugs and we sat together for a family autopsy.

"It's not right," said my mother. "Your children should outlive you. That's how it's meant to be. You shouldn't live longer than them."

She shook her head, as if in disbelief.

"I'm so sorry," I said. "I wish there was something I could do."

"Don't worry about doing anything, Brad," said my Mum. "Just being here is a big help to us."

"That's right lad," my Dad said.

Even though I was nearly sixty, my Dad still referred to me as 'lad'.

Their grief made me feel guilty, truly guilty.

I didn't have a great deal of guilt over what I'd done to Brian. It was mainly the effect that Brian's death had on my parents that troubled me.

I decided to make it up to my parents as best I could by writing a really good obituary for my brother. I composed it as soon as I got home that evening.

He only merited a bought-and-paid-for two-line entry like the average person gets, something along the lines of 'Much loved son and brother; he will be greatly missed'; but the next day, I managed to swing it with one of the sub-editors to give him a half-page. This was the day after the news of his death had broken.

He'd worked as a lowly dogsbody of some kind for a co-operative food wholesaler. However, he fancied himself a writer, and he'd had some of his work published in the sort of magazine you've never heard of. I made more of this in his obituary than you would have believed possible.

There was, for a start, a quite sickening photograph of him in his best writing pose, pen in his upraised hand, while staring meaningfully into the heavens. This took up a quarter page.

Plus I wrote a whole load of baloney about how he'd been one of the nation's leading (but largely unrecognised) writers. I concluded with words expressing how tragic his early demise had been, robbing the country as it did of the flowering of his talent, at a time when he was producing his best work;

it was an irreparable loss; that kind of thing. I didn't mention that the only person who recognised his talents was himself, and that he probably read his own stories to give himself a hard-on while he tossed himself off.

As soon as that issue of the Manchester Daily News rolled off the presses, I visited my Mum and Dad and gave them a copy, open at the page of my brother's obituary. They were both highly impressed, and grateful to me for writing it. I felt myself glowing with pride at their comments.

"It really does our Brian justice. It's the best thing you've ever written," said my Dad.

This was an exaggeration, but I knew what he meant. It was a well-crafted piece of work, even if it took far too many liberties with the truth.

My Mum was equally fulsome.

"You've used a very good picture of our Brian," she said. "He looks so distinguished and handsome. I'm going to cut your article and the picture out of the paper and have it framed professionally, and hang it on the wall in the front room."

Then she burst into tears.

I must confess that I had mixed feelings where Brian's death was concerned. Yes, I was glad to be shot of him. On the other hand, I did feel a certain sense of loss, I'm not sure why. I think I may have missed having a hate object.

The meeting with my parents had been a huge success for me. I left their house with a warm glow. But I was soon brought down to earth. Shortly after I'd returned home, a police car pulled up outside the house.

32

Two burly coppers got out and marched up the drive. There was a tall middle-aged one with a burgeoning waist and a shit-sweeper of a moustache, and a younger, slimmer, well-scrubbed one. They both stopped next to my car, which was parked on the drive, and looked closely at the wheels. Rather too closely for my liking. Then they knocked on the front door.

"Bradley Sharpe?" Asked the older one when I opened it.

"That's me," I answered. "You can call me Brad. How can I help?"

"We're making some enquiries, sir, about your late brother. Can we come in?" His tone was almost apologetic. It didn't fool me.

"Of course," I said.

I led them through the hall and they joined me and Sandra in the front room.

"Sorry to be troubling you at a time like this. We just have a few questions to ask you, if you don't mind." He looked me in the eye. "Did your brother have any enemies to your knowledge at all, sir?"

I shook my head.

Apart from me, no, I thought. *But there must have been plenty. He must have rubbed a lot of people up the wrong way, knowing him.*

"None that I can think of," I told him.

"Was he involved in drugs?"

I looked suitably pensive.

"He used cannabis many years ago. But he hasn't touched the stuff for at least two decades."

He scribbled in his notebook.

"Did your brother have any involvement with Satanism, Mr Sharpe?"

I feigned surprise at this question, even though I was the individual most responsible for propagating the theory that Devil Worshipers could have been responsible for the murder of my brother.

"Good Lord, no."

He scribbled again.

"Did he have any involvement with any secret sects of any kind?"

"I think he was a member of the local fiction-writing group."

"That's not what we're really looking for, but I suppose it may be significant. What was your relationship with him like, Mr Sharpe?"

The loaded question. They'd been saving it. I couldn't see any point in lying.

"Not very good, although I did make an effort to get on with him for our parents' sake. I thought he was a bit of a prat, to be honest with you."

"That wasn't what you wrote in that newspaper you work for."

"Well, you know what obituaries are like. They're meant to show people in the best possible light."

They both nodded.

"Of course, sir. I couldn't help but notice that all the tyres on your car seem to have been replaced recently. Is there any particular reason for that?"

A rush of adrenaline flooded through my body. I forced myself to breathe deeply.

"They were slashed," I replied, "It was an act of pure vandalism." (That was true).

"Did you report it to the police, sir?" The younger one asked.

Damn, I thought, *I should have done that.*

"No, I'm afraid I didn't." I said.

The coppers looked at each other.

"Why not sir?"

"There didn't seem to be much point," I told him. "That kind of criminal always seems to get away with it."

They shook their heads in unison. They were like a pair of synchronised swimmers.

"Well, you should have reported it, sir. Even if we don't catch them for your crime, it helps to have that kind of thing on record. We might catch them slashing someone else's tyres, then we could get them prosecuted for more than one offence."

I looked apologetic.

"Sorry, you're right."

"We need to eliminate you from our enquiries, Mr Sharpe," the older one said. "We believe your brother died on the night of the 20th of March. Can you tell us what you were doing on that night?"

"My memory isn't that good," I said. "I'll have to look in my diary."

I checked and Sandra did the same.

"I stayed in all night," I told them.

"That's right, he did," Sandra agreed. "I remember now. We were together all night. I had a bit of a lie-in the next morning."

This seemed to satisfy the police, at least for the time being. They both closed their notebooks, and said goodbye, and went on their way.

After they'd left, I reflected on the fact that they hadn't mentioned Brian's affair with Sandra. I wondered if they were keeping this information up their sleeves for the time being, intending to confront me with it when they had other evidence that would put me at the quarry where Brian had been found.

33

Not too long after that, the Coroner released Brian's body and we had an intimate family and close friends funeral for him.

My parents went through another period of grieving, and I publicly provided them with the sort of loyal support that only an eldest son can give.

During the funeral dinner afterwards, my Dad got a bit drunk and took me to one side.

"Look, lad, there's something I've got to tell you." Because of the brain damage he'd suffered during his heart attack, he spoke with a slur, but at least his mental faculties didn't seem to have been compromised. And he was on the mend. "Your Mum and me," he continued, "we've been to see a solicitor. We had to. We had to sort out our Brian's affairs. Anyway, Brian didn't make a will, and we're going to inherit everything he had. But we don't want it, lad. We're both in our eighties now, and it's no use to us. We want you to have it all. The lot."

He handed me a business card with the name and address of a prominent Manchester solicitor on it.

"We'd like you to go see the solicitor and

arrange everything. Do what needs to be done. And make sure the solicitor gives it all to you. The lot. You can tell him we'll sign what we have to, so that we can make sure you get it all. Is that all right, lad?"

"Yes Dad. Of course. Whatever you and Mum want."

Every cloud has a silver lining.

And that wasn't all.

My work on Brian's Obituary did more for his reputation than I could possibly have anticipated. Shortly after it was published, I received a telephone call.

"Is that Mr Bradley Sharpe?"

"Yes. Please call me Brad. How can I help?"

"My name is Jeremy Oakley. I'm the commissioning editor at Express Digital Publishing. I've been shown a copy of the obituary you wrote about your late brother Brian. Tragic story, by the way. I was wondering if you'd be able to email me some of his work, with a view to putting together an anthology, if it passes muster."

"I'd be delighted."

There was a memory stick in Brian's flat with enough stories on it to fill a dozen anthologies. I sent them by email to Jeremy Oakley.

We swiftly concluded a deal with me, as the beneficiary of Brian's estate, entitled to receive all the royalties from the anthology when it was published.

Due to the unifying theme of angst that ran throughout Brian's stories, the publishers gave the book the title *Living with Demons*.

I waited and waited for the police to question me on the subject of my brother's relationship with

Sandra. It never happened. Then one day I took a call from Jed.

"Brad," he said, "Can we meet up please? I need to talk to you."

That made me shudder.

Anyway, I agreed to the meeting and went to his office as soon as I could.

34

"Listen" he told me, "those photos I took of Brian and your Missus, I ought to hand them in to the police."

My stomach jumped. I nodded. And gulped. And tried hard not to appear anxious.

"But I've given it a lot of thought," he continued. "Did you ever show your copies of the photos to Sandra?" I shook my head. "And did you have it out with Sandra about her affair with Brian?"

"No I didn't," I replied. "I was going to, but then all this came up, so I've decided to let it go."

"Have you destroyed the prints I gave you?"

"Yes."

He looked relieved.

"I know it can't have been you who killed Brian, and if I tell the police about his affair with Sandra, it won't help to catch the murderer," he said. "All it'll do is cause you problems, and send the police in the wrong direction. It might actually help the murderer, because the police will divert resources into investigating you that would be better employed in pursuit of the real killer. So I'm going to wipe those photos from my system. And neither of us will mention anything about it ever again."

I could have hugged him, but I didn't want to look too pleased. A rush of relief flooded over me that I fought hard to keep to myself.

"No, of course we won't. Thanks Jed. That's much appreciated."

With the sensation of walking on air, and a smile on my face that lasted for the rest of the day, I left his office.

I had the distinct feeling that things were going my way.

And I was right.

In the short term, at least.

35

At some point it became apparent that the police investigation into Brian's death had stalled.

The Skull Crusher seemed to have gone into retirement, and my life had entered a new happy period, enhanced by the odd tingle of excitement at the prospect of passing a few minutes of the day with Kimberley Jones, whose attentions, I admit, I found most pleasing.

It was as if I had embarked on my own personal renaissance.

But then, just when everything seemed perfect, something happened to ruin it all.

36

My mobile rang as I got out of the shower. Cursing, I answered it. I always felt a need to answer my mobile come what may, just in case there was something that genuinely couldn't wait, such as a medical emergency involving the kids.

The voice at the other end was unfamiliar and sinister. It was obviously altered by some form of technical wizardry and had a synthetic quality to it.

"Mr Sharpe, is that you?" The voice asked.

"Yes, this is me, Bradley Sharpe," I replied.

A silence lasted for a few seconds, then:

"Bradley Sharpe, Newspaper Columnist?"

"Yes. What do you want?" I asked impatiently.

Water was dripping from my wet body onto the bedroom carpet. I hadn't had the chance even to give myself a perfunctory dry with the towel before taking the call.

Another silence.

"Mr Sharpe, I have a proposition to put to you."

I wondered what could be going on. Whatever it was, my instincts told me it wasn't likely to be good.

"What exactly is your proposition?"

"That you pay me a very large sum of money to keep me quiet."

I felt lead weights spinning around the pit of my stomach.

"Quiet about what?" I asked, although, of course, I knew.

"Quiet about what you did."

I had to confirm the worst.

"And *what*, exactly, did I do?" I demanded.

"The Skull Crusher Murder," said the voice.

My hands trembled slightly. I hoped my speech didn't also have a tremble to it.

"How much do you want?" I asked.

"I've been doing some checking up on you. It seems you've come into some money from your late brother's pension scheme and his death in service benefits. That will be enough to keep me quiet."

I should cocoa. That package was worth in the region of £100,000, and I had plans for it.

Looking back on things, I should have asked the blackmailer what evidence he had of my involvement in my brother's death, and I should have bargained hard for him to hand it over on payment. But I was new to the world of the criminal, and I didn't have a criminal mind, so my reaction was as innocent and guileless as yours would no doubt have been, in similar circumstances.

"All right," I said. "What do you want me to do?"

"I want you to get the cash ready. I'll call you again to let you know how to get it to me."

The line went dead. I didn't bother trying to find what number I'd been called from. I knew that the exercise would be futile. Instead, I embarked on an equally futile course of action: ceaseless worry.

I worried about what exactly my tormentor knew and how he knew it; about who he was, and where he was; and, worst of all, I worried that once he'd been paid, he would simply ask for more money, and then more, until I was completely ruined, and then he would rat me out to the police.

Shortly after receiving the blackmail call, I watched Crimewatch with Sandra. This is a show I normally view with interest, as it provides material for my Crime Chronicle columns. However, tormented as I was with apprehension that evening, I couldn't concentrate on it – not until a young and extremely attractive member of the Greater Manchester Police appeared and asked the public for help in connection with the unsolved murder of Brian Sharpe.

I sat up and listened intently at that point, fearful that she might divulge some morsel of information that could lead to my arrest.

She showed the viewers something I hadn't seen or heard about before: a grainy black-and-white video of a man wearing a hoodie who was entering Brian's apartment block. Sometime later, the shadowy figure emerged with Brian in tow. The police wanted this man to come forward so as to eliminate himself from their enquiries. He never did.

As I watched the video, I squirmed with discomfort in my chair, even though I knew I could never be identified from it. My face was hidden from view in the film, just as I'd planned, and moreover, I've always espoused the opinion that men of my age look ridiculous when they wear garments like Hoodies; so no-one would ever suspect me of having one.

Nevertheless, I felt uncomfortable at seeing my

image linked with the murder of my brother on national television. It was too close for comfort.

I spent the next day (in between bouts of fretting) trying to think of something positive to do.

The only plan I could come up with was getting hold of the money that I needed to pay off the blackmailer and then paying him off. This would likely do no more than buy me time, but it was all I had.

Because I was new to the blackmail scenario, I didn't bother trying to call the bank about getting hold of my money, I just joined the queue at the tills.

Eventually I made it to the counter and in a low voice I said:

"I'd like to withdraw a hundred thousand pounds in cash please."

The girl behind the laminated glass screen raised her eyebrows to a point somewhere near the middle of her scalp, but, to her credit, she didn't betray any other signs of surprise.

"You'll need to give us twenty-four hours' notice," she said firmly. "And bring with you two forms of proof of identity. A passport or photocard driving licence, together with a utility bill or Council Tax bill with your name and address on it."

All I could do was confirm the arrangements with her, which I did, before I made my exit.

When I got home, Sandra was poking about in my wardrobe. She used to do that kind of thing from time to time. It's not that she was nosey; she just liked things to be orderly, and she knew that I was incapable of keeping my clothes tidy enough to meet with her exacting standards.

She turned to me as soon as I entered the bedroom.

"What's this?" She asked, holding out a bulging plastic carrier bag. "I found it at the back of your wardrobe."

37

S he opened it and looked inside.

"There are some of your dirty clothes in it. And shoes," she said.

I ran up to her at a pace that would have done justice to a world-class sprinter in an Olympic final, and as casually as was possible under the circumstances, I took the bag from her hands.

"It's just some old stuff I was going to give to one of the charity shops," I told her.

I hoped to God that she hadn't noticed anything suspicious in there.

The next day I took the bag to the Oxfam shop on Oldham Street. I knew that they'd give everything a good cleaning, and I nurtured the hope that some poor sod would buy the stuff, and line himself up as the prime suspect in the murder enquiry.

Straight after that, I collected the blackmail money. I had to meet with a couple of members of the bank staff in a back office and watch as they counted it. Then I had to count it myself, and confirm that I agreed it was all there. Finally, I had to sign a disclaimer so that if I was mugged and lost everything,

I couldn't sue the bank for giving me that amount in cash.

I'd requested the money in fifties. They were presented to me in bundles, which I managed to stuff into the many pockets of the ski jacket I was wearing.

The sight of £100,000 in cash is inspiring. It is a sum that ordinary folk such as you and I do not often get to see in bundles of £50 notes. The sight of those wads of cash brought home to me even more than the loss of the figure on my bank statement just how big a sum the blackmailer was extorting from me for his silence.

It made me wonder if I could get away without paying.

I didn't know what evidence of my crime the blackmailer might have had at his disposal, but supposing for the sake of argument it was the photographs taken by Jed, what did they prove? Not guilt, just motive. The police would still have to build a case against me. But if the blackmailer gave the photos to the police, it would be like stirring up a hornet's nest. They would redouble their efforts, and maybe come up with something else.

No, I could not risk that. I had to acquiesce. I had to pay.

And that presented its own problems.

If I did pay, what if there was a future police investigation into my affairs? Would the fact that I'd withdrawn £100,000 from my bank, for which I was unable to account, be incriminating? ("Ace crime reporter Brad Sharpe takes £100,000 cash from his bank and claims he doesn't know what he spent it on. Was this the bung that was used to silence the blackmailer who knew Sharpe had murdered his own brother?").

My brain was buzzing with possibilities, none of them good. So I took a couple of aspirin. They didn't help.

Kimberley came and sat next to me (I was at work at the time) and said:

"You look a bit unhappy Brad. That's not like you. Is there anything I can do to cheer you up?"

I looked at her full lips (enhanced with the most unfeasibly red lipstick I had ever seen) and thought to myself, *yes, I can think of a few things*. Then I forced a smile.

"I'm fine, thanks. I'm not really unhappy. It's just that sometimes when you're involved in reporting crime, it gets to you that people can be so inhuman at times. I'll get over it in a few minutes. I always do."

She crossed her legs. I heard them crossing even above the din in the office. It was as if my ears were especially attuned to that sound – a suggestive slur of nylon upon nylon. It sent my heart all of a-flutter and for an instant I forgot my woes.

"Well, if you want to talk, I'm always here for you, Brad," she told me.

I felt my eyeballs moving in a direction somewhere south of her trim waist and ordered them to stop. It was like trying to stop an oil tanker; they had a momentum of their own. Somehow I managed, but when I did, I found that they were focused directly on the inviting chasm that lay between her breasts. I rubbed my eyes.

"I must be tired. Thanks for that, Kimberley. You're a good friend."

I tried not to dwell on how good a friend she might be willing to be.

In the days that followed, I felt like a sheep offering up its throat to a man wielding a carving knife. It began to get to me.

I shouldn't be so passive, I told myself. *I ought to be doing something to improve matters.*

But what?

The only course of action open to me was to try to work out who the blackmailer was, and to remove him from the picture. But I knew that wouldn't be easy. I'd found it impossible to remove Jed Barker from the picture, even though I was desperate to prevent him from revealing my motive for killing Brian. Would I be any more able to kill my blackmailer?

And, quite apart from that, there was the practical difficulty of finding out who the blackmailer was. I had nothing to go on beyond a telephone call from an unknown number.

Still, I was not without my suspicions.

While I had no evidence that it was Jed, I kept thinking that it could be no-one else.

I asked myself: how many people other than Jed knew that I had a motive to kill Brian?

There was only Sandra, but she didn't know I'd found out about her affair. And even if she did know, she wouldn't blackmail me. It would be totally out of character. If she did anything, she would go to the police.

My mind kept returning to two critical issues: Jed was the only person who knew I had a motive to kill Brian; and he'd always shown an interest in money that verged on the unhealthy.

He'd told me that he was going to destroy the

photographs of Brian with Sandra, but maybe he had just said that to put me off the scent. In reality, he might have retained them and bided his time. And when it became clear that the police enquiries were going nowhere, the time was ripe to use what he knew to part me from my money.

I had always thought of Jed as someone who shared my own moral code – I saw him as someone who, like me, might duck and dive a bit to get things done, but who was, like me, on the side of the Angels when it came to the crunch. Now I wasn't so sure.

I tried to point my suspicions in another direction, but there was no other direction available. Logic dictated that the culprit had to be Jed.

The second telephone call came when I was reading a bedtime story to Jack.

38

Jack was four years old and still at the age where I read to him every night when I tucked him up in bed. Lucy was seven, and I would have thought that she would have grown out of it, but she always insisted on having a story too.

Some years before, there had been a sale of stock from the Manchester Library. It'd enabled me to buy hundreds of children's books for a song.

Now, every night at bedtime, I pored over them for suitable stories to read to the kids.

I found myself increasingly turning to the classics such as Little Red Riding Hood and Hansel and Gretel. Stories that involved blood and gore, but had a happy ending. I was able to put my heart and soul into reading stories like that, and both the kids loved my performances.

It was while I was starting to read something or other from the Brothers Grimm to Jack that my mobile rang. I pressed the button to take the call, at the same time as I read out the words "Once upon a time". Then I put the mobile to my ear. A familiar, if distorted, voice asked for me by name.

"Just excuse me for a moment, Jack," I said. "Daddy has to take a telephone call."

Jack looked pissed off, but he didn't grumble.

I went into the main bedroom.

"Once upon a time," the caller said, "there was a very bad man who killed his own brother and had to pay a lot of money to keep it quiet. Have I got your attention, Brad?"

"One hundred per cent," I replied.

"Good. Have you got the money for me?"

"Yes."

"All £100,000?"

"That's right."

"Very wise. Think of it as an investment in your own future. Now listen carefully. I want you to put the money in a holdall. Tomorrow I'll call you again and tell you what to do next. Be ready with your holdall. Got that?"

I wondered where I could go to get a holdall at short notice.

"Yes, I've got that."

"Oh, and one more thing, Brad."

"What's that?"

"Don't try to fuck with me."

"No, of course not. I wouldn't dream of it."

The line went dead. I felt annoyed that I was having to hand over £100,000, annoyed that I would have to buy a new holdall to do it with, and even more annoyed at the bullying way I'd been spoken to.

I wanted to vent my rage at my Blackmailer for putting me into this position. In fact, I wanted to vent my rage at the whole world for putting me into this position. But I had to restrain myself. Rage would achieve nothing, except drawing unwanted attention to my actions. So instead of allowing my rage to boil over, I put it onto a low flame and left it to simmer. It joined any number of pots and pans of bile that I was already keeping nice and hot for any unfortunate individual who came my way at the wrong time.

The next day I put my cash into a brand new holdall, and I found out that the trouble with having £100,000 in a holdall is that you can't let it out of your sight.

I set off to work with the holdall in the car, but then I got to thinking about what I would do when I got there. I couldn't leave it in the car, that was for sure. And if I took it into work, I'd have to carry it around with me wherever I went, including the toilets and editorial meetings. That would never do. So I turned around and headed back home, sat at my pc with the holdall at my side, and emailed my colleagues to inform them that I was working from home. I didn't bother giving them any explanation for this course of action. I reckoned they'd assume it was all part of the grieving process which, to date, hadn't manifested itself. Then I spent a couple of hours oscillating between boredom and apprehension while waiting for the call from my blackmailer.

By the time it came, I'd worked myself up into such a state that I jumped into the air when my mobile rang and almost dropped it.

"Brad, it's your new friend speaking," said the strangely mechanical voice.

"Oh yeah, I was wondering when you'd call."

"Have you got the money ready like I told you?"

"Yes, in a holdall, just like you said."

"Good. Drive to Platt Fields Park. Wait in your car near the main entrance. You'll hear from me.

You've got twenty minutes to get there. If you're late, the deal is off."

I knew that Platt Fields Park was twenty minutes away, and then some. I shot out of the house and set off as if I was in a drag race, jamming my foot on the accelerator so hard that the tyres smoked before the car launched itself forward and screeched down the road. I'd forgotten that I was in a twenty mile an hour zone. By the time I remembered, I'd driven over a speed bump at such a velocity that I'd catapulted myself upwards and banged the top of my head painfully against the roof of my car.

That knocked some sense into me. I realised that no purpose would be served by having a crash or being arrested, so I slowed to a sensible pace and disobeyed speed limits only when it seemed prudent to do so.

Some twenty-five minutes later, I reached the main entrance to Platt Park. There was nowhere to park my car, so I pulled up on some double yellow lines. Then I sat wondering whether my Blackmailer would carry out his threat to cancel the deal because I was late. I was being naïve. I should have known that the lure of money would easily overpower a mere five-minute delay.

My mobile rang. I fumbled in my pocket and somehow got it out without dropping it a second time.

"What kept you?" The Blackmailer asked.

My mouth was dry. It was difficult to answer.

"I did the best I could," I croaked.

"All right. Get out of your car and walk along the main path with your holdall. Head towards the other end of the park. Don't dawdle."

"I'm parked on double yellow."

"Then you'll get a ticket and pay a fine. Now get on with it."

You Fucking Pillock, I thought. *I'm going to fucking have you. You see if I don't.*

I grabbed the holdall out of the back and got going. My pace was brisk and I was soon panting. My arm became numb with the effort of holding a bag full of cash, so I transferred the holdall to my other arm. That one became numb too. As usual, I cursed myself for my physical weakness and lack of fitness. Why hadn't I started going to the gym like I'd promised myself when I'd learned how hard it was for me to swim across a small lagoon?

The main thoroughfare took me past an ornamental fountain, then a war memorial. As I passed the war memorial, my mobile rang again.

"On your left you'll come to a small wood. There's a path between the trees. Follow it."

I saw the wood and took the path. It led to a rectangular car park flanked on all sides by thick bushes.

My mobile rang again.

"You'll see a grey saloon car. Go and open the boot and put your bag in it. Shut the boot and walk back the way you've come. Don't turn around. If you do, the deal is off."

I glanced around. There weren't many cars to choose from, and only one was a grey saloon. I went up to it and tried the boot. It was unlocked, so I opened it, dropped in my holdall, then slammed it shut. I heard the car lock. Someone must have been nearby, watching me from the bushes. Whoever it was had locked the car with a remote key fob immediately after I'd shut the boot.

As ordered, I walked back the way I'd come. When I entered the cover of the trees, I heard a car door open then slam shut, heard the engine fire up, and the crunching of gravel as the car pulled out of the exit at the other end. Soon the sound faded into nothing, taking with it my £100,000.

I wondered when the next demand would come, and how much it would be for.

My mobile rang again.

"Is that Brad?" It was the mechanical voice of the blackmailer.

"Yes," I said, with some apprehension.

"I wanted to say thank you, Brad."

"Think nothing of it. You're welcome." I said, through gritted teeth.

"Sarcasm doesn't suit you, Brad," said the voice. "Anyway, there's another thing I wanted to tell you. I'm rather disappointed that you don't seem to have worked out who I am. Bye-bye for now."

39

Those words chilled me to the marrow. Especially the "for now" bit tagged onto the end of his farewell. Did that mean he was going to come after me again?

I determined then and there to nail him, whoever he was.

And I thought I might have a means to do that.

When I'd gone to the blackmailer's car, I'd focused all my concentration on it, and memorised the make and model of the vehicle, and the registration number.

As soon as I got back to my own car, I wrote down the details: "Grey Ford Focus YO09 UPV".

Then I looked up and saw a ticket on my windscreen. I'd been fined for parking on double yellow. That was £100 I'd never see again, I reflected bitterly. As if I hadn't already lost enough money that day.

It was in a state of deep angst that I drove into work, the only relief from which was the thought that the blackmailer might leave me alone for a few weeks before making another outrageous demand.

Unless, that was, I could take him out before the demand came.

"What's the matter Brad? You don't look too happy today."

It was Kimberley, bless her.

"It's nothing," I told her. "I've just lost some money, that's all. I've been given a parking fine. I don't know why I'm getting so upset, it's only £100. It must be the injustice of the thing that winds me up."

She put her hand gently on my shoulder. Her touch crackled with some unknown force that I found irresistible.

"Ouch," she said. "I know how you feel. It's so galling to get one of those tickets. You're playing it down, but £100 is a lot of money. How about having a drink with me after work, to help you cheer up?"

My mind raced with obscene possibilities. I told it to behave itself.

"That's great, I'd love to Kimberley."

We went to the local Wetherspoons. Kimberley wasn't driving and had a couple of gins with tonic. They were the sort you get during Happy Hour – the size of a triple for the price of a single.

There was an old man in a grubby suit propped up against the bar. He smelled of piss. If you can put up with rubbing shoulders with the worst that society has to offer, Wetherspoons is a good place to go for a drink.

She soon downed her two gins, and I bought her a third. At those prices I could afford to. And anyway, the day had cost me so much already that an extra few quid seemed neither here nor there.

I don't recall what we talked about. It was mainly Journo stuff.

One thing that did stick in my mind is that after her second drink, Kimberley looked me straight in the eye and said:

"You'd make the perfect boyfriend."

I'd only had a couple of halves of bitter at that point, so I wasn't about to get over excited about that statement. But I have to admit that it played on my mind.

Anyway, I packed her off in a taxi and went home to Sandra.

"You're late," she said, as I walked through the door.

"Sorry," I told her. "I was feeling wound up, so I had a drink after work."

"Who with?" She asked.

"Kimberley Jones, the new Women's Features writer."

"Should I be jealous?" She asked, smiling.

"Yes, I'm about to embark on a reckless and passionate affair," I told her.

She laughed again, and so did I.

Then, after I'd put the kids to bed and done a few chores, we sat together and watched television. Well, Sandra watched television; I sat next to her, feigning interest in the television, while contemplating my next move.

I decided that I more or less knew the blackmailer and Jed Barker were one and the same person, and I would have a meeting with him just to confirm what I already knew.

Then I would do him in.

40

The next day I called him.

"Jed, there's something I'd like your opinion on."

"Fire away Brad."

"I really need to discuss it in person."

"Okay, I'm free this morning so you can come right over if you want."

After driving to the Northern Quarter and parking at the back of his office block, I made my way to his flea-bitten office on the top floor. He buzzed me in and I sat down on the uncomfortable chair that he reserved for his clients.

"Hi, Jed. There's something I've been meaning to ask you," I said. "It's kind of difficult to talk about."

He could tell I was more serious than usual. He sat up a little straighter in his chair.

"What is it, Brad?"

"Those photos we discussed a few weeks ago. Did you get rid of them?"

His cheeks coloured a little.

"Yes I did. They're gone."

I could tell he was lying. I leaned forward slightly as if taking him into my confidence.

"There's something else," I said, "about Brian. You don't – you don't—"

"Yes Brad?"

"You don't secretly think I had anything to do with Brian's death, do you?"

He widened his eyes.

"Of course I don't. If I thought that, the police would be looking at those photos right now." he said, with a tell-tale stress tremor in his voice.

"Thanks Jed," I told him. "That means a lot to me. Before I forget, there's another MDN job I want you to look at. There was a crime committed the other day. I need you to trace the car. It's a grey Ford Focus, registration number YO09 UPV."

I looked at his face so hard I swear to God I could see the individual pores on his skin. There was nothing, not so much as a flicker in his expression, to give anything away. Was he carefully controlling his reactions? If so, he was a master at it.

"I can do that for you right now," he said.

He poked rapidly at the keyboard on his desk.

That was when I saw it – the faintest hint of a smile at the corners of his mouth. He tried to suppress it, but he didn't quite manage. It was as if he was having a laugh at my expense, finding humour in a private joke about me. Well, I had a private joke of my own that would wipe that smile right off of his face.

"The plate doesn't belong to a grey Ford Focus," he continued. "It's a plate that doesn't exist. Someone must have had it made up at a bent garage. What was the crime?"

I tried to conceal the level of my interest in his facial expression.

"It involved the theft of a large amount of cash in a holdall," I said.

He hesitated before he answered.

"Strange," he commented. "Why would anyone be carrying cash around in a holdall? Was it a bung or something? Was someone being blackmailed?"

I felt as if he was toying with me in some way, that he was playing a game of cat-and-mouse in which he had cast himself in the role of the cat.

Well, we'll see about that, I thought.

"It might have been a bung," I said. "Or a bribe." Then I stared him directly in the eye. "Or even, as you suggest, blackmail money."

"Who's being blackmailed?" He asked with faux innocence.

"No-one you know. And it's only a theory."

I allowed myself a sly smile at this point.

There was no hard evidence to go on, but my instincts told me that the culprit was Jed, and my instincts are seldom wrong. He was my Prime Suspect, indeed my only suspect, and he would have to go.

I regretted not having disposed of him before, when I'd had the chance. In my imagination, I replayed that moment in Brian's flat where I'd held the statue above the back of his head. Had I brought it down on him then, I could have spared myself a lot of heartache and £100,000. It didn't bear thinking about.

Now I'd have to start all over again with getting rid of him, and I didn't see how it would help me to get my money back.

Then it occurred to me that if I were to put Jed's head in a vice he might be inclined to tell me what he'd done with the money. I could just tighten it up a bit and ask him. Then, after he'd told me everything, I could tighten it up some more and put an end to him and his annoying activities.

Given the amount of misery Jed had inflicted on me, plus his theft of a substantial sum of my money, and the general level of his treachery, it seemed perfectly reasonable that I should take drastic measures against him. It was a form of natural justice in a situation where the legal system was unable to help me.

I began to feel distinctly enthusiastic about the project that lay ahead.

41

My plan called for me to pretend that I had yet more MDN business for Jed, and I set up a meeting with him to discuss it just before lunch the next day.

I asked him if he'd like me to bring a sandwich up to his office for him, and he said yes. I took us both some sandwiches and bottles of fizzy water. Jed's sandwiches and fizzy water were laced with enough GHB to stun him, and he was soon snoring in his chair. That wasn't at all what I'd wanted. I'd somehow miscalculated the dose. I had intended to put him into the same passive dreamlike state that Brian had been in when I'd kidnapped him. It would be impossible to do that with Jed. He was too far gone. I would have to improvise. And I would have to improvise quickly.

I went on a speedy shopping expedition and returned armed with a man-sized trunk and a sack cart. I'd made a few holes in the trunk to provide ventilation. In the interests of concealing my identity, I was wearing blue workman's overalls and a flat cap.

I tied Jed's wrists together then did the same thing

to his ankles, took his car keys, packed him into the trunk, and manoeuvred him out of the building on the sack cart. We ended up at the back of his car.

This was when things got tricky. That's what happens when you're not a career criminal; you take on tasks for which you're ill-prepared, because you don't think like a true criminal.

Jed drove a saloon rather than an estate, and I found it impossible to get the trunk into the boot. It was far too heavy for me to manage on my own.

As I struggled, the driver of another car observed my efforts. He was young, strong, and fair-haired. He got out of his vehicle and walked towards me. He was wearing a navy suit. I wondered if he was a plainclothes policeman and felt something akin to panic.

"Would you like a hand?" He asked.

I tried lamely to disguise my voice with a cod North-Eastern accent.

"Thank you, I would." I said.

"Are you from Northern Ireland by any chance?" He asked.

"Newcastle," I replied tersely.

Then I bent down to hide my face and grabbed a handle at one end of the trunk.

"Sorry," he said. "I'm not very good with accents. I'll take this end." He grabbed the other handle.

His end of the trunk came up from the ground easily and he hefted it onto the lip of the boot. My end came up with rather more difficulty and he had to help me get it high enough. Between us, we manoeuvred it inside. The effort left me gasping for breath and streaming with sweat beneath my overalls.

I wondered if my innocent helper would be able

to identify me, and prove to be my undoing. Naturally, I considered hitting him over the head when his back was turned and lobbing him into the boot, along with the trunk. But this was no more than idle fantasy. I couldn't bring myself to attack an innocent man, and anyway, there was nothing to hit him with. Had there been, I confess things might have been rather different.

"There, you're all sorted," he said proudly.

I was half expecting him to say something like: "That was heavy, have you got a body in there or something?" But he didn't.

The trunk was too big for the boot, so I used bungee ropes to hold the lid shut.

"Thank you," I said, in what I supposed to be a gruff workman's voice. "You've been a big help."

"No worries," he replied. "Glad to give you a hand."

He disappeared into the building and I set off in Jed's car.

I parked it out of sight in the garden of the Old Chapel then hurried a few streets away on foot and took a taxi back to work.

I spent the rest of the day gleaning information from the local police to use in my crime column. When evening came, I went home as usual and had dinner with Sandra and the kids. I told her that I'd be going out later for a drink with a work contact who had a story for me. I read some Brothers Grimm to the kids and tucked them in. Finally, I returned to the Old Chapel where I'd left Jed in the back of his own car.

It was parked where I'd left it, and the trunk was still in the boot, secured with the bungee ropes.

I donned my overalls and got the sack cart at the ready, Jim's modified one for transporting bodies. Then I opened the trunk and somehow dragged Jed up out of it and manhandled him onto the cart. He was showing signs of coming round, but still had no strength to move his limbs.

I wheeled him down the steps into the darkness of the cellar then hefted him from the sack cart onto the wooden chair. He slumped in it, his head on his left shoulder, with his wrists tied behind his back. I crouched down and untied his ankles, then bent him forwards and untied his wrists. I pushed him back into the chair and sat him up in preparation for strapping him in.

At that moment I had the funny feeling I was being watched by a single unseen eye. It was as if Brian's missing eye was hidden in the cellar observing me. It was most disconcerting. I raised my head and looked around, but saw nothing I hadn't seen before.

Moving a limp body around is extremely hard work and I stepped back for a moment to wipe the sweat from my brow with a tissue.

Jed's eyes opened and he leaped from the chair like a Jack-in-the-box.

His hands fastened around my throat, and he rammed me backwards across the cellar floor until I was pressed up against the wall. I could feel my larynx being compressed. I couldn't breathe. I grabbed his wrists and tried to relieve the pressure.

He'd tricked me and got the better of me.

How had I let *that* happen?

He was smaller than me, but younger, probably fitter and stronger, and there was no escape.

I lashed out wildly with my knees and feet, but

even though I made contact, he didn't seem to feel it. In desperation I let go of one of his wrists and thrust my hand at his face. My finger caught him in the eye, and he loosened his grip. I somehow pushed him away and he lost his footing on a slippery part of the floor, and landed on his back.

He immediately rolled onto his stomach and got onto his hands and knees so that he could stand up again. That gave me just enough time to snatch a piece of wood from the table and whack the back of his head with it. He lay on the ground groaning while I reflected on the fact that the new plan had become a reprise of the old plan – the one involving the statue at Brian's apartment.

In his weakened state, Jed was unable to resist. I forced him back into the chair and this time I made no mistake. I fastened him in and tightened the vice until his head was stuck quite fast.

My heart rate was dangerously high by this time, so I left him strapped to the chair and went upstairs to try and relax. I made a cup of tea and sat for a while, breathing deeply. As I sipped at my tea, I reminded myself of Jed's infamous behaviour towards me, and of the fact that he had skanked me out of £100,000.

The recollection of what he had done put me in a very bad mood indeed.

When I went back to the cellar, I was quite calm, but in the very highest of dudgeons. It was what you might call a cold fury.

"Now then," I said. "What have you done with my money?"

The blow I had hit Jed with must have been very painful, but it didn't appear to have had any lasting effects. He was fully conscious and I could tell that he was considering the question I'd just put to him.

"What money?" He asked after a while.

"You know what money," I said.

He looked as if he was trying to shake his head, but because it was stuck fast, it stayed quite still and his shoulders rotated from side to side.

"I don't," he insisted. "I don't know what you're talking about."

I didn't bother to answer. I tightened the jaws of the vice.

"Do you know now?" I asked him.

"NO!" He shouted. I loosened it.

"Better try and remember," I said.

His eyes narrowed.

"You're the Skull Crusher Murderer. I knew I should have taken those photos to the police."

If his fate had not been sealed before, it was certainly sealed then, in that moment.

"That's very astute of you, Jed. But then, you always were rather insightful. That's why I've used your services so many times. That, and the generous payola scheme we introduced to sweeten the MDN contract work. Anyway, now that you know how grave your situation is, perhaps you'll tell me where you've hidden the money."

When a person has his head in a vice, it is not always possible to tell what expressions are flitting across his features. In Jed's case, however, there was no question that the expression on his face was one of extreme distress.

"I remember now!" He shouted. "Your money is in the safe in my office. If you just take me there, I can get it for you."

I felt vindicated. He'd confirmed that he was the Blackmailer. Moreover, he had given me what I required – the whereabouts of my money. I determined to show him no mercy, and began to tighten the jaws of the vice.

"Tell me the combination of your safe and the alarm code for your burglar alarm," I said.

He volunteered the information most readily. I wrote it down. Then I continued winding the handle of the vice.

The action stiffened against the resistance of his head, then his skull gave way with the same sort of sound that a jar of marmite might make in similar circumstances. Turning the handle of the vice became suddenly easier.

Next I applied the Brace and Bit to the top of his head. Soon, his dense hair got caught up in the bit and became a tangled mess. I had to wrench hard on the brace to pull it out by the roots before I could really get going. When it came to my next victim, I would shave the head before applying the brace and bit. But with Jed, I was still learning my trade, as it were.

It didn't take long to finish the grim business at hand.

Afterwards I cleaned myself up and went home.

When I got there I sat in front of the television wondering where to dispose of the body.

Something told me the lagoon at the bottom of the quarry where Brian had been found would be the best place. After all, the commonly held view is that lightning never strikes twice, so the police would be unlikely to expect a second body in the same location as the first.

The next day I used Jed's car to transport his body

to the quarry, weighted it down by securing concrete blocks to his ankles, with shorter chains than before so as to eliminate the possibility of his head bobbing to the surface the that way Brian's had done, and I threw him over the edge of the drop. I made sure that his trajectory would take him wide of what was left of the wooden platform.

He entered the water with a satisfying splash.

I drove his car to Speaker Woods on the outskirts of the city and set fire to it.

And that was the end of Jed.

The loss saddened me. After all, he had been more than a work colleague. On the other hand, I was heartened by the fact that I'd rid myself of the horrors of blackmail, and the threat of exposure.

Now I just had to deal with the easy by comparison peripheral stuff.

42

The next day I visited Jed's office wearing my flat cap and armed with his key and the codes he'd given me. After first availing myself of the protection of a pair of surgical gloves, I unlocked the door, went inside, and disarmed his alarm system. His landline started ringing but I ignored it. It rang repeatedly.

With a fast-beating heart, I opened the door of the cupboard in which he'd hidden his safe, and unlocked it using the combination I'd got from him. Then I looked inside.

It contained a loaded revolver, a clip of bullets, a couple of memory sticks, and a brown envelope.

So this is what he had planned for me if I'd taken him back to his office to open up his safe, I thought. *A bullet in the head. It's a good thing I put paid to Jed when I did.*

There was £1,000 in the envelope, mostly in twenties. I pocketed it, and wondered what he could have done with the other £99,000.

I'd taken bag of Heroin from the Old Chapel. I put it in the safe next to Jed's gun and bullets. It made for a nice little montage. I was sure the police would hatch a great many theories about it, none of them correct.

I carefully closed and locked the safe. That damned telephone started ringing again; again I ignored it.

After taking the lift to the ground floor, I walked towards the exit with my head lowered and my flat cap pulled down right to my eyebrows. A woman walked past me. It was Melanie, Jed's wife. She seemed distressed. Luckily, she didn't recognise me.

I hurried to the back street where I'd parked my car and made a clean getaway.

When I got home I checked the memory sticks. Both of them contained incriminating photographs of Brian with Sandra. No wonder Jed had turned pink when I'd asked him if he'd got rid of them.

I wiped the memory sticks clean, then for good measure smashed them to pieces with a hammer and threw them in the bin. I wondered how many more copies Jed might have made and whether any of them were on the hard drive of his computer. The thought occurred to me that I'd have to return to his office and check his computer, or even remove it for analysis with a lump-hammer. I put on my coat and headed back.

When I got there I found Melanie in Jed's office staring at his computer screen. I dared not think what she could be looking at.

"Hello Melanie," I said. "I've come to see Jed."

She rotated the scroll button on the mouse.

"He doesn't have you in his diary today," she said.

"I've just come on the off chance of catching him," I told her. "Is everything all right?"

She shook her head. Then tears began to run

down her face and she sobbed. She looked rather odd. From the eyebrows down, her face was contorted with grief; but above the eyebrows, it remained smooth as a sheet of ice, and equally immobile.

"What's wrong, Melanie?" I asked.

She tried to tell me but she couldn't speak. It took her at least five minutes to get to the point where she could tell me. Then when she started talking, I noticed how full her lips were, far more full and sensual than I'd remembered them.

"It's Jed," she said, in between bouts of sobbing. "He didn't come home last night. And he didn't warn me he wasn't coming home. He always tells me, even if he's only going to be late by a few minutes or so. I haven't heard from him since yesterday morning. Something's wrong and I know it, Brad. Something is terribly wrong."

I began to feel queasy because of Jed. He had brought his death on himself, but I didn't want Melanie to suffer. I liked her. I'd met her quite a few times in the past. The Barkers had taken out the Sharpes for a number of expensive meals to cement Jed's informal contractual arrangement with me – the one that had led to me supplying him with MDN investigative work. I'd found her to be good company. And good looking, too.

There is something particularly moving about a good-looking woman when she's upset. I did my best to comfort her.

"I'm sure he's away on a job or something, Melanie," I reassured her. "He probably just forgot to tell you, that's all."

It was a lame thing to say, and no more than a reprise of what I'd said about Brian under similar circumstances, but it was the best I could come up with at such short notice.

"No, he would have told me," she said emphatically. She scrolled the diary again. "He was expecting you for lunch yesterday. Did you see him?"

I wondered how to answer. For an instant, I thought the unthinkable: that Melanie might have to follow her husband to a watery grave.

Cursing my ineptitude, I wondered why I hadn't thought to check Jed's diary and wipe from it everything that could give me away.

Because I'm not a real criminal, that's why not, I thought, and I lamented my lack of a criminal's acumen. It could lead to my downfall.

What should I tell Melanie? I wondered. If I told her I hadn't visited Jed, it might be that I would get away with it, because I'd entered the building incognito. On the other hand, I had no knowledge of what the security cameras might have picked up, and it was possible that I could be identified, flat cap and all, as the person who had last seen him alive.

After a few seconds of deliberation, I plumped for denial. It was a high-risk strategy, but so was every other strategy I could think of.

"I didn't see him," I told her. "My plans changed at the last minute, so I never came round here yesterday."

She stared at the computer screen as if it ought somehow to disclose more than it did.

"I tried to tell the police that Jed is missing but they weren't interested," she said. "They won't even *consider* him as missing until he's been gone for forty-eight hours. By that time it might be too late."

I wondered when she would learn that it was already too late.

In a way, I hoped that the information would emerge swiftly, the quicker to put an end to her anguish over where he might be. And I admit, I wondered if there might be a human-interest story to be told when details of Jed's fate became known. A story that looked at the activities of the Skull Crusher through the eyes of a grieving widow. It might be worth fifty column centimetres or so.

"Maybe I should take a look at what's on the computer," I volunteered. "You never know. A fresh pair of eyes might see something that you missed."

She stood up.

"Yes, all right then, you sit here. I'll search amongst Jim's papers," she said.

I took her place in front of the computer screen and found his folder of photos. I didn't bother checking them; I just deleted the lot, lock stock and barrel, then I deleted the contents of the recycle bin for good measure. In the meantime, Melanie ferreted around in the cupboard where the safe was hidden. I heard her opening it.

"Oh my God," she said. "What's this?"

I stood next to her and looked in the safe myself, as if for the very first time.

"Do you mean the gun?" I asked.

"Yes, and this."

She held up the bag of heroin I'd hidden there earlier.

It didn't surprise me that Melanie hadn't known about her late husband's gun. Many husbands keep secrets from their wives. Complete transparency is seldom a feature of any marriage, partly because of the need of one spouse to spare the feelings of the other. Jed had probably been trying to protect Melanie from worrying about the hazardous nature of the work he was sometimes called upon to do. For instance, some of the assignments I'd given him had involved illegally tapping into the communications of Manchester's celebrities to provide scoops for a colleague who penned the gossip column. Had Jed been rumbled, he might have ended up in jail.

Anyway, the revelation that her husband – her late husband, but she wasn't to know that at the time – owned a gun troubled Melanie, particularly when combined with the revelation that he had a stash of Heroin in his safe.

"What is it?" I asked. "Not drugs, surely."

She nodded.

"I think it is. I think it's Heroin. What would Jed have been doing with Heroin?"

I assumed the manner of a man who wouldn't stoop to questioning the integrity of a friend in his friend's absence.

"I don't know," I told her, "but there's got to be an innocent explanation for all this. Better put the heroin back in the safe and lock it up. If Jed doesn't turn up and you have to call in the police, they'll need to see all the evidence there is."

She placed the Heroin back where it'd been and shut and locked the safe.

"Would you like to come for a drink?" I asked her. "I have to be back at work soon, but it might help you to be with someone for a while and talk about things."

She wiped the tears from her cheeks, smudging her carefully applied blusher.

"Thank you, Brad. I'd like that," she replied.

176

We went round the corner to the Marble Arch, a nice old-fashioned pub, and I bought her a spritzer. I had a pint of bitter myself. I felt as if I needed one. If I hadn't had to work that afternoon, I would have drunk several.

We spent about half an hour together, during which Melanie explained to me how much she loved Jed, how much she missed him, and how worried she was about his disappearance.

She wasn't the only one who was worried. While I felt that I'd eliminated the immediate threat of Jed blackmailing me, deep down I had the uneasy feeling that things might be spiralling out of control, and that something could emerge from the woodwork at any moment that would bring my world crashing down. Chief amongst my concerns were the photos.

But at least, I told myself, I was doing my best to manage the situation.

I don't know quite how, but Kimberley and I ended up in bed together soon after that.

43

It just seemed a natural progression from having a drink after work. I was feeling pleased as a result of having taken my fate in my own hands, and Kimberley could perhaps sense it, and she put temptation before me.

What's more, I had the keys to Brian's flat – my flat – and it made everything very convenient for us. It was so easy to go from the pub, she slightly sozzled, and me slightly less so, to the apartment.

"We must do this again sometime," she said, as I shoved her into a taxi afterwards.

"Yes of course," I replied, making a mental note not to.

I felt pangs of guilt about having had sex with Kimberley, as I'm not one for cheating on the matrimonial relationship, but I reminded myself that Sandra had cheated on me, and that made me feel better. It was almost justification for what I'd been up to.

And I was on a high.

Higher, if truth be known, than I'd been for years, maybe than I'd ever been before.

I felt as if I'd discovered the secret of eternal youth.

Only a few months before, I'd been knocking on the door of old age. At the age of fifty-nine, I only had one year left during which I could call myself middle-aged. In a few months' time I would turn sixty, and then I would have to call myself Old.

Sixty.

That is the official arbitrary age at which you go from middle age to old age.

On my fifty-ninth birthday I'd been in such a tizz about it that I'd consulted Google on how best to postpone Old Age. Google had made several suggestions about what I could do. All of them, from exercise to Viagra, promised to improve my looks and re-invigorate my sex life.

How effective would any of these remedies be, I wondered, as compared with the miraculous effects of killing people who you don't much like? Or who just get in your way?

Yes, my own homespun remedy for old age had improved my looks, personality, libido and confidence. Even my skin looked better. It was just unfortunate that my remedy was not one that could be readily shared with others in need of rejuvenation.

As I went about my business, I felt better and better with each passing day.

Then Jed's body was discovered, and my world began to implode again.

44

I must have made a mistake with the chains. At any rate, they'd come loose from Jed's ankles, and his body, full of the gases of decomposition, had risen to the surface of the lagoon. It was discovered floating face down, by a group of children who ought to have had something more constructive to do with their day, such as playing on computer games in the comfort of their own homes.

When the police picked me up for questioning, it came as a surprise, even though I was half expecting it. Two of them came up to me while I was in the car park outside work. I was grateful they hadn't had to go in and detain me in front of my colleagues.

It was two plainclothes coppers who approached me. I wondered if that meant they were treating me as a higher priority suspect than before.

One of them had a forehead that reached to the back of his neck. He had unsuccessfully tried to cover it with a few wiry black strands pressed into service from around his ears.

"Mr Bradley?" He asked, producing a warrant card.

It identified him as Detective Inspector Desmond Adkins. I reflected that there was no need for the warrant card. Anyone could see that Adkins was a policeman, even though he wasn't in uniform. That's the thing about plainclothes officers. Their idea of plainclothes is just another obvious form of uniform. It made me wonder why they bothered calling it plainclothes.

His colleague, an earnest young black man, also showed me a warrant card. It identified him as D.I. George Blake.

"That's my first name," I said. "I'm Mr Sharpe. Bradley Sharpe. You can call me Brad."

In print this probably gives the impression that I responded in a calm manner, however I was anything *but* calm. I felt my chest tighten as I replied. My breathing became shallow. I had to force myself to take long deep breaths. I could only hope that Adkins and his colleague wouldn't notice the anxiety they were causing me to feel. There is something about being accosted by a policeman even when you're innocent that gets to you. And I was not innocent. I suppose there must have been a massive stress distortion to my voice. I tried to hide it by feigning a cough.

"Mr Sharpe, you are under arrest on suspicion of murder," said Adkins.

Those words "under arrest on suspicion of murder" sent chills running up and down my spine, and I felt myself weakening at the knees, as I had done decades before as a child when the school bully had challenged me to a fight.

There was no point in arguing with them, so, when told, I got in the back of their car and tried to compose my thoughts. I rehearsed in my head the lies I would have to tell if particular lines of enquiry came up. They were lies I'd rehearsed many times before, but practice makes perfect.

The journey took longer than I expected. I realised after a while that this was because we weren't going to the local police station that I knew. I was being driven out of town. This may have been because word had got around that I was a well-known figure in the city centre Nick, and a decision had been taken at some higher level that I ought to be interviewed at an unfamiliar venue, by policemen that I was unlikely to have met before. Whatever the reason, it disturbed me. All the police I have known in the course of my job have been personable and talkative. But these two, Adkins and Blake, were different, as was the Custody Officer who booked me in at the police station. They were, to a man, professional, cold, and aloof.

Add to that the fact that I was possibly staring at a murder charge and was in unfamiliar surroundings, and you can imagine the apprehension I felt.

I was briskly ushered into a cell and told to wait.

"Is this really necessary?" I asked as the Custody Officer pulled the door shut. "I'm not going to run away, you know."

The last few words of my sentence were drowned out by the sound of the door slamming and the key turning in the lock.

I soon discovered that a large part of life as an Accused consists of waiting. This may be a deliberate ploy on the part of the police. *Keep them waiting,* they probably think, *and there's more chance that they will cough.*

Alone in the cell with my thoughts, I breathed deeply, and sat patiently for a while, playing the role of the model Accused. Then I decided I'd had enough, and made up my mind to exercise my right to have legal representation.

The door to my cell had a small square aperture at head height with vertical steel bars set into it. When I looked between these bars, I could see the custody Officer and he could see me. He was a large shaven-headed man with slack lips and a bored expression. I pressed my face to the opening and shouted at him:

"I want to see a lawyer!"

He looked up from some papers he was perusing and nodded. Reassured, I sat down again and waited.

Half-an-hour later, I made the same request of the same officer, somewhat tersely this time, and he nodded again. Half-an-hour after that, when no lawyer had presented himself, my mood changed from angst to annoyance, then from annoyance to anger. I stood in front of the opening a third time and vented my spleen on the Custody Officer.

He walked over to me from behind his desk.

"There's no need to get like that, sir," he said calmly. "I'm sorry you've been kept waiting. This is a busy station and we're short staffed. Now do you have a solicitor to represent you, or do you want me to get the Duty Solicitor?"

I was fuming from the experience of having been shut in a cell for one and a half hours for no constructive purpose.

"Do I look like a common criminal?" I snarled. "Do I look like the sort of person who has his own fucking criminal lawyer on hand to represent him whenever he is fucking well accused of murder? Of course I want the fucking Duty Solicitor!"

The custody Officer looked more infuriatingly bored than ever as he listened patiently to my outburst.

"Of course, sir. I'll arrange that for you, if you don't mind waiting."

I returned to my seat – an unforgiving wooden bench set into the wall – in a somewhat overwrought state. Their ploy of keeping me waiting had had the opposite effect to that which they'd intended. Far from making me cowed, it had resulted in my becoming agitated, and determined to enforce my rights.

After a few minutes of fuming I stood up and shouted through the barred aperture:

"And I want the telephone call I'm entitled to make! And I want it now!"

The custody Officer brought over a telephone. I had to reach between the bars to use it.

"No need to shout sir," he said in mellifluous tones. "You could have just asked."

His manner would have tested the patience of any saint.

I called Sandra.

"Sandra, it's me, Brad."

"Whatever are you doing?" She asked. "Your Dinner is ready. Do you want me to put it in the oven for you?"

"Just leave it on the worktop or something. I don't know when I'll get home."

"Where are you?"

"You're not going to believe this. I'm in a police station. In a cell, would you believe? I've been accused of murder. These idiots actually seem to believe that I could have killed someone. I don't know how long they're going to keep me here. I've already been waiting for two hours. They should be out looking for the real killer, instead of wasting my time and theirs on this farcical exercise."

"What did you say?" She asked. She sounded as anxious as I'd been earlier. "Did you say they think you killed someone?"

"Yes. I've been accused of murder."

"Murder of who? Not your Brian, surely."

"They haven't said who, but it could be him they have in mind."

"Oh, I'm so sorry for you Brad. That must be very trying for you."

"It is. I'll see you as soon as I can. Say goodnight to the kids for me."

"Of course Brad. I love you. See you later."

"Love you too. See you."

Since the re-launch of our relationship we often said "love you" to one another. It was a very positive development.

I hung up and the Custody Officer returned with the telephone to his lair behind the counter. I had no option other than to wait yet again.

After a while, a key turned in the lock, the door opened, and a burly Irishman walked in. He was carrying a brown leather briefcase, and wearing a reassuring smile. He extended his large beefy hand and introduced himself.

"I'm Frank Maloney, the Duty Solicitor. I'm told you require my services."

I relaxed a little. Knowing that someone was coming in to bat for me was reassuring.

"That's right," I said, "I haven't got a solicitor except for the one that drew up my Will years ago. I don't think this would be his cup of tea."

"Probably not, Mr Sharpe. Let's take a pew, shall we?"

We both sat down on the unyielding wooden bench and Frank opened his briefcase.

"Now would you like to tell me whether there is any substance to the police allegations?"

I struck up a pose of outraged innocence.

"There is none whatsoever," I declared. I was tempted to add: "It is nothing more than a farrago of lies," but I felt that would be over-egging my denial.

Frank nodded.

"Very well then, I will represent you on the basis that you are innocent. Before I do, I'll have to ask you about a number of matters that the police have disclosed to me. These are likely to come up in questioning. I need to know in advance how you intend to respond."

He took some notes from his case and consulted them.

"So, firstly, would you like to tell me what you did when you received the news that your brother Brian had been having an affair with your wife?"

The answer came naturally to me, having been tried and tested in my head many times before.

"What do you mean?"

"The police have photographs that prove that your brother was having an affair with your wife. They pulled them off the hard drive of a computer that belonged to an acquaintance of yours, a Mr. Jed Barker. Someone had tried to delete them. What was your reaction when you were told your wife was having an affair with your brother?"

Shock spread like a plague across my face.

"Oh my God," I said. "It can't be. Sandra having an affair with Brian." I cupped my head in both my hands. "It can't be."

"Are you telling me you didn't know that your wife was having an affair, Mr Sharpe?"

I looked at Frank's face through the gaps between my fingers to see if it looked like he believed me. He seemed convinced.

"That's right. This is the first I've heard of it," I said.

"And you haven't seen any photographs of your wife and your late brother together?"

I sobbed, quite realistically.

"No, and I'm still not sure I believe you."

"I'm sorry to be the bearer of bad news, Mr Sharpe, but there is photographic evidence which leaves no room for doubt. Your wife and your brother were having an affair, and that could be construed as giving you a motive to have killed your brother. But if you are saying you never had sight of the photographs, and you knew nothing of the affair, then that puts paid to that allegation. I'm sorry about bringing it up, but I had to put it to you because the police are going to do exactly the same."

He asked me a number of other questions about issues that potentially linked me to the murders, then the door opened, and the Custody Officer stuck his head round it.

"Mr. Sharpe, everything's ready for you now," he said, as if I was in a physician's surgery waiting to see the doctor. "Come this way."

We followed him into what I discovered was an interview room. It was only marginally less grim than the cell had been, and was sparsely furnished with a table, four chairs, and a recording device. We made ourselves as comfortable as we could on two of the chairs.

The Custody Officer left us, and Adkins and Blake came in. After giving me a curt nod, they sat down opposite Frank and I. They were both stony-faced, and, I felt, trying to appear intimidating. It worked. I had a rush of adrenaline that made me feel jittery.

Adkins switched on the recording machine with a remote control device and dictated the date and time and persons present at the interview, then began questioning me.

"Mr Sharpe, you called in sick at work the day after your brother died. Shortly afterwards you called in again and said that the tyres on your car had been slashed and that you needed your car urgently to work on a story. How was it that you were too sick to go into work, yet you were well enough to go out in your car to work on a story?"

After being kept waiting for so many hours I was feeling angry and defiant as well as stressed.

"I thought this was a criminal investigation not an Employment Tribunal." I snapped.

I left it at that. I decided it was up to the police to press me to get the information they wanted from me. I wasn't going to volunteer it, not after having gratuitously been kept waiting for two hours.

"Please answer the question Mr Sharpe," insisted Adkins. "I repeat: how was it that you were too sick to go into work, yet you were well enough to go out in your car to work on a story?"

It was a tricky one, but fortunately I had a prepared answer.

"I don't see that what I tell my employers has anything to do with you," I said," but if you must know, I ate something that disagreed with me. I felt better later in the day."

My voice trembled when I answered but I knew it wouldn't be long before I would settle down, and my voice would return to normal.

"It's a bit of a coincidence, Mr. Sharpe, that the murderer left tyre tracks all over a muddy quarry that could lead to the identification of his vehicle, and the day after the murder took place, you found your tyres slashed and had to replace them," he said.

"My client does not have to opine on your speculation as to what does and what does not constitute coincidence, Mr Adkins," said Frank.

Adkins looked slightly rattled.

"I will ask you a direct question," he said. "Did you drive your car to the quarry where Brian's body was found on the day of his murder?"

"I will give you an equally direct reply: No I did not." I said.

Frank nodded encouragement. Adkins looked unconvinced.

There was a computer on the table between us. Adkins turned the screen at an angle so that we could all see it. He pressed a key on the keyboard, and we all watched the familiar footage of me entering Brian's apartment building alone and leaving it a while later with a clearly inebriated Brian in tow.

"The man in the Hoodie appears to be about the

same height and build as you, Mr Sharpe," said Adkins. "Would you agree?"

Frank leaned forward, looked at me, and shook his head.

"No," I said emphatically. "He has nothing in common with me; height, build or anything else."

"Is that person in the Hoodie you?" Persisted Adkins.

"No, it is not," I replied.

He played another video, this one showing a man in a flat cap and overalls entering the front entrance to the building in the Northern Quarter where Jed Barker had his office. This same man was shown leaving the building by the rear exit with a sack cart and a trunk, which, with the assistance of a member of the public, he hefted into the back of Jed Barker's car.

"Do you recognise the man in the flat cap, Mr Sharpe?" Said Adkins.

"No. I've never seen him before."

"He looks rather like the man wearing the Hoodie in the previous footage who resembles you, wouldn't you say?"

Again, Frank looked at me and shook his head.

"I don't make a habit of watching myself on video, so I really couldn't say," I snapped.

Adkins persisted.

"Are you the man in the flat cap Mr Sharpe?" He asked.

"No," I answered. "And I wouldn't be seen dead in a flat cap."

"You engaged Mr Barker to do some investigative work for you, didn't you, Mr Sharpe?" Said Adkins.

Without waiting for my answer, he pressed

another key on the keyboard and a series of images of Brian with Sandra flashed up. I did my best to look aghast, as if I was seeing them for the first time.

"Yes," I admitted in a quiet voice. "I engaged him to do some work for me."

"And that work was investigating your own wife to find out whether she was having an affair with your brother, wasn't it, Mr Sharpe?"

He asked this with an air of triumph, perhaps convinced he'd now pinned something on me.

"No. I thought she might be having an affair, but I had no idea who it might be with."

"When Jed Barker told you who your wife was having an affair with, and showed you these pictures, you lost control and decided to kill your brother Brian, didn't you Mr Sharpe?" He said.

I played my trump card.

"No. Jed didn't show me the pictures and he didn't say anything about Brian and Sandra," I replied. "He told me he hadn't found anything. He must have been trying to spare my feelings."

Adkins ignored me. He was determined to air his view of how events must have played out, irrespective of what I told him.

"When you killed your brother, you realised you would also have to kill Mr Barker because he had evidence of your motive, and he was in a position to finger you. Isn't that the case Mr Sharpe?"

Frank intervened:

"My client has already given his answer to this question, Mr Adkins. He has told you he had no knowledge of his wife's affair and that the late Mr Barker gave him no reason to have any knowledge of her affair," he said.

"That's hard to believe," sneered Adkins, "a private investigator who doesn't disclose the results of his investigation to a client in order to spare his client's feelings. Do you think a professional private investigator would really do such a thing?"

"I must object," said Frank. "My client doesn't have to answer that. It's nothing more than idle speculation."

Adkins referred to his notes.

"Interestingly, our technical team tells us that the attempt to delete these photographs from the hard drive of Mr. Barker's computer occurred the morning after Mr. Barker disappeared. His widow, Mrs Melanie Barker, tells us that you were with her in the office that same morning and you fiddled about with his computer."

Adkins gave me a hard stare when he said that. He thought he had me on the hook, but I knew I could wriggle free.

"I was trying to help her. I was looking for information concerning the whereabouts of her husband. I didn't delete anything."

"Then who did?"

"I must object a second time," said Frank. "My client doesn't have to answer that question. That is a matter for the police to find out. It would be idle speculation for my client to attempt to answer it."

"That's all right Frank," I said. "I'm willing to answer it. Mrs Barker herself might have deleted it by accident. Or someone unknown – the real murderer – might have done it. The man in the flat cap, for instance."

The two coppers looked at each other. Their

questioning had reached a dead end, at least for the time being, and they knew it.

"Gentlemen," said Frank, "my client has answered all your questions, and now you must put up or shut up. Either charge him, or let him go. Far be it from me to tell you how to do your own job, but I would advise you that you have insufficient evidence to substantiate a murder charge."

I had been vindicated.

Adkins nodded sadly. He dictated into the recording device that the interview was concluded.

"So I'm free to go?" I asked.

"Yes Brad, you're free to go," said Frank.

We filed out of the interview room.

"Any chance of a lift home?" I asked the Duty Officer. "I don't have my car with me."

He pushed the phone in my direction.

"I suggest you call a taxi, sir. We are the Greater Manchester Police, not a Taxi Service."

I got home at about 9.00 p.m. and heated up my dinner in the Microwave Oven.

While my food was being warmed up, I told Sandra all about my ordeal at the hands of the police. She was very sympathetic.

"As if you didn't already have enough worries Brad, what with Brian dying, and your dad being ill, and then Jed dying. On top of all that, you've had this to deal with."

After I'd eaten, I poured us both a whiskey, and we settled down on the sofa together to watch some television. Jenny the family cat leaped up onto my lap and meowed, as if sensing I'd had a hard time of it, and then she settled herself down for a good kip. Sandra played with my hair – the few pathetic tufts of it I had left at the sides of my head – and I began to relax after my latest ordeal.

But deep down, I was wondering how long it would be before the police would find a new piece of evidence with which to torment me, or indeed to convict me.

45

One good thing came of the discovery of Jed's body, the opportunity to write about it.

I went to town on the story. Two murders with the same M.O. make a serial killer. Even the police agreed. And so it was official: a serial killer was on the loose in Manchester, and the city was, or would soon be, gripped by panic. It wasn't just that the serial killer murdered people; it was the spectacular way in which he did it that made for great copy. It was as gruesome as anyone could remember any murder being. I devoted an ocean of ink to speculating – as tastefully as possible – what it must have been like for his victims as they approached their final moments.

(It would have been, for example: "grim and painful beyond words, beyond belief, beyond even imagination.").

I also analysed the twisted mind of the killer. Why had he used the quarry as a dumping ground for both his victims? Was it a part of his sick ritual? Or did he mistakenly believe that the police and members of the public wouldn't think to look for a second body in the quarry, because lightning couldn't strike twice in the same place?

I pulled out the photographs we'd taken following Brian's death, and I had one of them worked on, to compare the path of descent of the first body with that of the second. Two black dotted lines illustrated the different trajectories both bodies had taken. It showed how the killer had improved on his methods since his first killing, how he had learned from his mistake of throwing the first victim onto the wooden platform and had aimed the second several yards to the left of it, causing the cadaver to hit the water cleanly "like a diver taking the short cut to the surf in Acapulco Bay."

It made for gripping copy. The MDN flew off the shelves that day.

Jack Baines, the elderly sub-editor who edits most of my work came over to me after he'd read the story. He was close to retirement.

"Nice copy, Brad, very nice," he said.

He had a shock of white hair and a grizzled smoker's face.

"Thanks Jack," I replied. "From you, that's high praise indeed."

It was. Jack seldom had anything good to say about the writing of any reporter on the MDN. And he reckoned that anyone under the age of about forty couldn't write at all.

46

It wasn't long before Jed's burnt out car was discovered in Speaker Woods.

The fire had purged it of all forensic evidence, but perhaps offered more clues as to the workings of the mind of the Skull Crusher.

I duly set to work acquainting my readership with the significance of the find: it was probable the victim had been kidnapped in his own car, and readers were therefore advised to take special care when going to their parked cars, especially at night, and especially when there was no-one else around.

Happy as I was with earning plaudits for my crime columns, I could not help but harbour misgivings about it all. There was one key question that vexed me: what had Jed done with my money? Could it be traced back to me?

Another concern I had was with the way the National Press was reporting Jed's death.

I felt I knew better than anyone what the murderer must be like, yet the Nationals were giving over reams of paper to speculation about what kind of a person he was, almost as if he worked for them, and not for the

MDN. But ultimately I had to smile about it, as no-one could possibly confuse the sick portrait they painted, with that of Bradley Sharpe, respectable family man.

When the Greater Manchester Police forensic team had finished their work in the quarry, I had a word with Kimberley.

"How would you like to visit a crime scene today?" I asked.

"That's a fantastic idea Brad," she replied. "I'd love to. I'm free later this morning. Where is it?"

"The quarry where the Skull Crusher disposed of the bodies of his victims."

"That's fantastic, I can't wait."

I looked at her feet. They were shapely, I remembered, and usually in heels. They were in heels that day.

"It's very muddy in the quarry. You'll need some different footwear. We'll buy you something more suitable before we go," I told her.

Before we set off in my car, I took her to Top Shop where I'd noticed they were selling a range of women's Wellington boots that year. I'd done my research.

She looked them over.

"Which ones do you want?" I asked.

She put a finger to her chin and knitted her eyebrows.

"You choose," she said at length.

I decided on a pair called the Boops – they had Betty Boop emblazoned on the sides of them. With her big eyes, black bob, and sultry looks, the cartoon figure reminded me of Kimberley somewhat.

She took off her stilettoes and tried them on. She

was wearing black stockings. I could see the red of her painted toenails through the translucent fabric and felt a frisson of excitement. Even her feet were capable of driving me wild with desire.

"These are perfect," she declared.

They were a size three. Kimberly was tiny, like Sandra.

I paid up and we left the store with the Boops in a bag. It was the most unusual love gift – if I could call it that – I have ever bought.

When we got to the quarry, there was a clear blue sky and the sun was shining. Even though it was a weak winter sun, Kimberly massaged moisturiser with a high SPF over her face and hands before opening the door of my car. She was very careful when it came to sunlight. She said it had an ageing effect. What was her opinion of sleeping with an old man like me? To someone like her, it must have been like sleeping with Death.

She took her Boops from the Top Shop bag and put them on, I donned my black workman-style wellies, and we went for a walk, ostensibly for me to show her what crime reporting was all about; in reality, it felt more like some sort of assignation.

I had parked near the top of the rock face. We walked together to the edge of the sheer drop.

"This is where the Skull Crusher must have been standing when he threw his first victim down the cliff," I said.

"That victim was your brother, wasn't it?"

"Yes."

She gave me a comforting hug.

"This is where he must have been when he threw

the second victim over the edge," I told her. "See those tyre tracks? They could be his."

"It's so gruesome. But somehow fascinating. I can see why you do this job."

We took a stroll around the rim of the quarry. It was quite scenic, with views of the undulating Cheshire countryside in the distance, beyond the quarry workings. Then we descended a narrow path to the level of the lagoon.

"See over there?" I said. "That's the wooden platform my brother landed on when he fell. Thankfully he didn't feel it. He was already dead by that time, God rest his soul."

"Does Brian's death upset you a lot?"

"It does sometimes, when I dwell on it. But I try not to. And when I'm writing about the murderer, I try to keep a professional distance. It's as if I'm two people, the bereaved brother and the Crime Reporter. The Crime Reporter is the only one allowed to be present when I'm writing." (I didn't mention the third person inhabiting my body and thoughts – the Skull Crusher). "One of the reasons I'm devoting so much time to the story is to help the police. If I can raise enough awareness amongst the public, someone who knows something useful might come forward which will help to convict the killer. Then I'll feel I've done my bit to help avenge Brian's death, and he'll be able to rest in peace."

That was quite a speech, I thought. Kimberly seemed to think so too.

"If Brian could only know what you're doing for him, he'd be very grateful," she said. "And I'm sure your parents must be very appreciative," she added.

She seemed to admire Bradley Sharpe the

Fearless Crime Writer. I must admit, he was an individual I rather admired myself.

"Thank you. I like to think so. It's the least I owe Brian and my parents, now that he's gone," I said. "I'll tell you another thing I'm doing. I'm hoping to keep his memory alive by bringing out a book of his short stories."

She pricked up her ears when she heard this. She was an English Lit graduate and very interested in poetry and literature.

"Your brother was a writer?" She asked.

"Yes, and a very accomplished one at that," I told her, bending the truth to breaking point.

"Will you show me some of his work?"

"I'll do better than that. I'll let you have a signed copy of the book when it comes out."

I picked up a pebble and skimmed it across the calm surface of the lagoon. Then we took turns at skimming pebbles. She looked into my eyes, and for some reason we both started laughing and I took her in my arms. We enjoyed a lingering kiss in the winter sunshine next to the lagoon where the bodies of both Brian and Jed had been found. When I opened my eyes I noticed the sun shimmering on the glassy surface.

After we kissed, it seemed natural to walk hand-in-hand around the quarry and follow the footpath that led onto a nature trail through the surrounding trees. If it had been a hot summer afternoon, we might have had sex al fresco in the woods, but instead we returned to my car and headed back to work, and I wondered how long before we'd be in bed together again.

47

When I got home I found Sandra had arranged a babysitter for the kids. It was a teenage girl we knew from down the road, the daughter of one of our neighbours.

"I've decided we're going out tonight," Sandra explained. "We've been under so much pressure. We both deserve a break. We need to let our hair down."

I wasn't about to argue.

"Where are we going?" I asked.

"A party. It's being held by a friend of someone at the Agency. It'll be a good do, they're loaded. Put on your glad rags. We'll have to set off soon."

When we entered the house where the party was being staged (a mansion at the posh end of Cheshire) I immediately regretted going. I didn't know anyone there, and was distinctly ill at ease. I felt as if I somehow wouldn't measure up, and wouldn't be interesting enough, or good looking enough, for the crowd that was there.

These were concerns that never seemed to affect Sandra, no matter where she went, probably because everyone found her good looking and interesting. As soon as we walked through the door, she began a conversation with someone she'd never before met in her life, while I sloped off to the kitchen to fill up with Dutch Courage.

Glass in hand, I returned to the front room and forced my features into an expression that I hoped might appear confident and worldly-wise. Probably I looked desperate, but fortunately there were no mirrors nearby to inform me of the truth.

As I glanced nervously around the room, a grey-haired man walked so purposefully towards me that I wondered if I'd done something to upset him.

"Hi," he said, extending his hand. "I'm Derek, pleased to meet you."

I accepted the invitation to shake his hand.

"Brad," I replied. "Pleased to meet you."

"You're the journalist aren't you?" He asked. "The one who's been writing in the Manchester Daily News about the Skull Crusher."

"That's right," I answered. "How did you know?"

"One of the other guests told me. She knows your wife. About this Skull Crusher character. I get the impression from your column there's stuff you know about him that you're not letting on."

My new friend is rather insightful, I thought. *Rather too insightful for my liking.*

I wondered if I might have somehow given away too much with some of the things I'd written. But not to worry, I had an explanation.

"Yes, unfortunately I can't tell my readers everything the police tell me about the case. When a crime as horrific as this is committed, you always get someone wanting to confess to it, just because he craves the fame and notoriety that attaches to being a

203

killer. If I published all the details I know, anyone could come forward and use them to pass himself off convincingly as the murderer. So the police always make sure that some information only the real killer could know about, is held back. That way, if an impostor shows up, they're able to ask questions which will catch him out, and establish that he isn't the real thing."

"Very interesting," said Derek. "But that's not all, surely. I get the feeling when I read what you've written, that, well, it's almost as if you know the guy. What's that all about?"

I think I might have gulped at this point, but I wasn't about to be caught out.

"I'm glad you asked. A lot of people must wonder about that. While I don't actually know the Skull Crusher, I studied Criminology to degree level, and I've spent my entire career writing about criminals. Add to that, that I'm a keen amateur psychologist, and you have the answer. I believe I know what kind of a person the Skull Crusher is."

He cocked his head to one side.

"Go on then, tell me. What kind of a person is he?"

I noticed that a small crowd of people had gathered and appeared to be listening in on our conversation.

"Okay, here goes," I said. "My experience tells me that the Skull Crusher is likely to be a white male in his early thirties. He's a loner and his only sexual outlet is power. He enjoys the feeling of having control over people. He has an engineering background and he's probably unemployed right now, or working in a menial job. He feels that he's entitled to have a better role in life than he actually has, and that people have conspired against him in some way to deprive him of that role. He's frustrated about having been denied the opportunities that should have come his way, hence his obsession with power. He's the sort of person who could have been the Managing Director of an International Corporation or a top politician if things had turned out differently."

I noticed from the corner of my eye that my audience was hanging on my every word. It was how people often reacted to Sandra, but seldom to me. If, I'm to be honest, never to me.

Another person asked me about the Skull Crusher, and I soon found myself taking questions, and dealing with them as if I was an expert. I suppose I was an expert on the subject of the Skull Crusher, more of an expert than I dared to let on, more of an expert than anyone in that room could possibly have imagined.

"Do you think he'll kill again?" Asked a young woman in a red cocktail dress.

"Undoubtedly," I assured her. "His type always does. Once they've experienced the thrill of killing once, it's only a matter of time before they need to kill again to satisfy the urge. You mark my words, the Skull Crusher will kill repeatedly until he's caught."

Even I couldn't have predicted how true that statement was.

My questioner's face somehow managed to register shock and respect at the same time. I felt like a celebrity on one of those shows called 'An audience with so-and-so'. You know the type. A famous so-and-so stands onstage, and is asked a series of easy questions by fawning admirers. He responds with unfunny anecdotes. I'd always felt that I could do that. And here I was, doing something very similar. I almost said: "Next question, please."

After my impromptu show had ended, Sandra joined me.

"I saw you just now, you big show-off," she said.

I put on my best *who, me?* Expression.

"What do you mean?" I asked.

"Preening yourself in front of all those people," she said. "You loved it, didn't you? Come on, admit it."

I felt myself reddening.

"All right," I said. "It was a nice feeling."

"My husband the big show-off," she laughed.

In the period that followed, I found that my opinion on the Skull Crusher was forever being solicited, albeit often in a rather apologetic way, due to the fact many of my questioners knew one of the victims was my own brother, and they were sensitive about my feelings on the subject.

Just not too sensitive to ask about it, which was quite refreshing, really.

When we got home I reflected on what had happened, and I have to admit I felt rather good about it. Good about life in general, in fact.

Yes, maybe even good enough to kill again, and feel that rush of power once more.

48

I was given some respite from the attentions of the police from an unexpected quarter – the Police themselves.

They called in the assistance of a criminal profiler to help with their investigations. As might have been expected, at least by me, he sent them up a blind alley.

I will be forever grateful to the psychologist who profiled the killer, as he provided me with material that enabled me to produce one of my best-ever columns. It lacked the sensationalism of my earlier pieces, as there was little gore to speak of. But the piece more than made up for this by the intriguing picture it drew of the Skull Crusher Murderer.

Everyone wanted to know what kind of a Fiend was capable of committing the crimes horrifying Manchester, and I was in a position to tell them, having been given a copy of the criminal profile, hot off the presses.

My column informed readers (amongst other things) that:

"It is highly likely that the Skull Crusher is a white male who lives alone, probably in rented accommodation. He will be of less than average height, no more than five feet five or five feet six inches tall, and in his early-to-mid-thirties.

He will be unemployed or work in a manual job, such as labouring, or filling supermarket shelves. But he will have qualifications of some kind, likely to be in the Engineering or Technical sector, and this accounts for his dexterity with workshop tools.

His frame of mind will be one of frustration and anger. Frustration because he will feel his talents have not been recognised, and anger because he assumes he is worthy of better things.

He is likely to have sadistic tendencies fuelled by these feelings of anger and frustration."

(I have to admit that certain of the Profiler's observations about the Skull Crusher were rather astute – I can confirm that the Skull Crusher has felt frustration and anger throughout his entire adult life and that *is* because his talents have largely gone unrecognised).

"He feels that other people have conspired to deprive him of the opportunities he deserves to achieve his rightful station in life."

(Again, a bull's eye for the psychologist!)

"He is a loner who finds it difficult to talk to the opposite sex and who might be a virgin."

(Tragically wide of the mark).

Happily, although the profiler was correct with one or two of his observations, the overall picture was of someone as far removed from me as it was possible to get. If you were to ask my wife, she would no doubt tell you I'm unable to put up a simple shelf, let alone deal with technical and engineering matters, or handle workshop tools with any degree of deftness.

I wrote a long article based on the profile which probably resulted in every young man in Greater Manchester, who lived alone, becoming a suspect, as far as his friends and neighbours were concerned.

We commissioned an artist to provide a representation of what the Skull Crusher might look like, using the profile as the basis for the drawing. It turned out that he looked like a very nasty piece of work indeed. A couple of the Red Tops followed our lead with artist's impressions of their own. We all made hay on the psychologist's profile, one way or another.

The day that edition of the Manchester Daily news came out, I went to Tesco to buy a new notepad, and I couldn't help but notice that every shopper in the store carefully avoided the aisles occupied by two young male employees who were stacking shelves that day.

I just hoped that my column wouldn't lead to a lynching.

Because of the profile, the police reviewed their files on men who were single and aged between thirty and forty, then they re-interviewed many of the suspects in the target age group. This was all very time-consuming for them, and by-and-large, it took the heat off me.

I reported on these developments, having learned of them from Bob Napper down at the local Nick. I hoped to give the people of Manchester reassurance that the police were taking measures that might lead to the capture of their persecutor.

Of course, the police are not stupid. They all

knew, as a result of the notorious Yorkshire Ripper debacle some decades earlier, that they shouldn't narrow the focus of their enquiries too soon. But the resources expended on pursuing suspects below the age of forty meant that there were correspondingly fewer resources available for the pursuit of those aged fifty-nine.

What's more, although the police had not *officially* narrowed their focus, they had *unofficially* narrowed it. Most of the coppers believed (according to Bob Napper) that the culprit had to be a young man. They found it inconceivable that anyone could suddenly become a sadistic serial killer in late middle age. Part of me felt like explaining to Bob that the Skull Crusher was much misunderstood, and that he was not a sadist. But that was one of many things I kept to myself.

In spite of the general consensus within the police force that the killer was a young man, there was one copper who didn't go along with the "below the age of forty" theory.

I heard about him from Bob Napper.

"You're not going to believe this, Brad," he told me, laughing fit to burst. "There's a clown in Fallowfield who's got the most crackpot theory you've ever heard."

I took out my notebook.

"It might be worth sharing with my readers Bob, what is it?" I asked.

His shoulders shook with mirth.

"You won't want to share this one with your readers," he said. "He thinks *you're* the Skull Crusher."

I managed a thin smile.

"That's absurd!" I said, putting the notebook away. "Who's the clown in question?"

"They call him Adkins. He's a D.I. He's let it be known that he's out to nail you."

49

As soon as I received the advance copies of *Living with Demons* – the anthology of my late brother's short stories – I gave one to Kimberley. She was thrilled.

How odd, I thought, that my brother had, for a period, ruined my relationship with a woman; and now, by an astonishing turn of events, had done the very opposite.

Later that day, I whispered to Kimberly:

"Do you fancy doing anything this evening?"

That was a private code that she immediately and correctly deciphered as:

"Do you want to have sex with me tonight?"

She looked up from her keyboard.

"Yes, I think I do. Quite a lot, actually. Meet you in the car park at six?"

We duly met and went to Brian's apartment. By this time I had installed a new bed. We headed straight for it without consulting one another. It was like painting by numbers. Kimberly and I had, after only making love once before, already reached the stage with our lovemaking where we didn't have to wonder what the other person was going to do; we were like a well-grooved double act. Before we began, she quickly peeled off her clothes, but not all of them; she knew I liked it better that way.

I helped her off with the final items of clothing, other than for her stockings and bra, as I like to see these decorations on a woman during sex. It is strangely arousing.

When I removed her panties, I noted, as I had done before, that her attractive triangle of jet-black pubic hair was set against an unusually white skin, smooth as alabaster. The image of that black triangle in a white setting had a great power over me. I often pictured it in my mind's eye during the day. Sometimes it got in the way of writing my columns. I'd come to realise the only means I had of exorcising the image from my mind was by contact with the real thing.

After we'd made love, we spent a while lying together, our heads on the pillow next to one another, not talking, just enjoying each other's presence. She turned to look at me and her hair fell to one side. I noticed a row of discreet stitch marks up near her hairline. They were expertly done, almost invisible.

I had assumed that Kimberly must be younger than Sandra, but had never enquired about her age. Now I realised that she was, in all probability, older, much older, but fantastically well preserved. Her body put mine to shame. It was firm and lean, the result of dancing, gym work, yoga, and tennis, she told me. Our relationship suited her perfectly in some ways. Given the amount of time she must have spent on personal maintenance, she wouldn't have been able to fit anything approximating to a normal relationship with a man into her busy life.

50

I got home late after my session with Kimberley. Not desperately late, but more so than usual.

Sandra was already prowling round the kitchen. I gave her a peck on the cheek.

"Sorry about the time, Love," I said. "I had to file an urgent story, and it took longer than expected."

"That's all right," she replied. "I know it's all in a good cause."

She was referring to the fact that I was determined to do as much as I could to bring Brian's killer to justice. Which I was, as long as I didn't incriminate myself in the process.

It amazed me in some ways that Sandra didn't suspect me of having an affair, or subject me to an inquisition of some kind. She'd had an affair herself. Didn't she recognise the signs?

Apparently not.

Perhaps she thought me too loyal to embark on one, which I was, back in the day. But not any more. Something had changed, obviously.

Sometimes I wondered who the real Bradley Sharpe was:

- Bradley Sharpe, faithful husband and family man;
- Bradley Sharpe, middle-aged Lothario;
- Bradley Sharpe, fearless crime writer; or
- Bradley Sharpe, the twisted madman known as the Skull-Crusher.

How these individuals could co-exist within the same body, I cannot explain. And how I avoided confusing one identity with the other, I do not know. All of these people were me, and at the same time, none of them were me.

Deep down, I felt I was fundamentally still the same person I'd always been: the honest and moral person that my father Stan had brought me up to be. I had just been forced, by events, into taking a few short cuts.

If you have ever taken a short cut, and most people have, you'll understand how easily one can be drawn into behaving in a way that seems totally out of character.

51

The kids had waited up for me, so I put them to bed, read their bedtime stories, then went downstairs and snuggled down on the sofa with Sandra. At last we could both relax.

"Thank God," she said. "I love those two, but it's such hard work when they're about."

I wondered if she had any idea how hard that work was for a man so many years her senior. A man, moreover, who had so many other commitments and worries to drain his energies.

"You're right," I agreed. "Whenever I hear someone who hasn't got children complaining about how hard he works, I always think to myself: *you don't know what work is, Mate, and God help you when you find out.*"

She laughed.

"That's so true. I've heard some of my singleton friends complain about how tired they are at the end of the working day. How would they cope if they had kids and their working day didn't finish till they'd put them to bed? They'd be knackered, like we are. Do you want me to pour you a glass of wine?"

"Yes please. Make it a big one."

While Sandra poured my wine, I turned up the volume on the television. We were watching Crimewatch. For me, it was a matter of professional interest (and latterly personal interest!) – while, somewhat amazingly, Sandra regarded it as good entertainment.

The Greater Manchester Police were using it to make a nationwide appeal for help with the Skull Crusher murders. They showed some grainy footage of a man in overalls and a flat cap transferring a large trunk into the boot of Jed Barker's car. He was being helped by a member of the public.

"If you are the man in the flat Cap," said an earnest and very attractive policewoman, "we would like you to come forward so that we can eliminate you from our enquiries. And if you are the man helping him, we would like you to come forward and assist us to identify the man in the flat cap."

I felt a little queasy when I heard that. My face wasn't visible on the video footage, but maybe the Good Samaritan who had helped me with the trunk had managed to see what I looked like. I couldn't remember exactly how well I'd kept my features hidden from him.

Later in the show, the presenters revealed that they had received several telephone calls in connection with Flat Cap Man. That news made me feel rather worse, so I gulped down my wine and got another big one. Sandra could see I was agitated.

"Has it been a hard day for you?" She asked.

It had, actually. I'd laboured long and hard on my crime columns, then serviced Kimberley good and proper after work. When I'd gotten home, I'd played with the kids, read them bedtime stories, and tucked them up in bed. Throughout it all, I'd been intermittently plagued with worries about being caught. It had been an extremely demanding itinerary, as you might imagine. But Sandra could not be informed about that, of course, not the whole of it, anyway.

"Yes, it has. My days all seem to be harder than they used to be."

"Is that because of the Serial Killer stories you keep having to write?" She asked.

I contorted my face into a sad expression and nodded.

"Yes," I said, "it's not healthy psychologically having to immerse yourself in that sort of information, and write about it. It tears me apart sometimes."

"Do you think you should take a break from it for a while?"

"No, don't worry. I'll be all right," I said bravely.

As long as no damning evidence comes to light, I thought.

Just as I was thinking this, my mobile phone rang.

"Brad Sharpe here," I said.

The voice that answered was a familiar one. It was the mechanical voice of my blackmailer.

"Hello Mr Sharpe," the voice said.

I tried to remain outwardly calm.

"Hello. How can I help?"

"I think you can guess," said the voice.

I jumped up and put my hand over the receiver.

"The reception isn't very good here for some reason," I told Sandra. "I'll try it in the kitchen."

"What do *you* want?" I demanded, as soon as I was safely out of earshot of Sandra.

219

"You know what I want, Mr Sharpe."

"How much?" I asked.

"Another hundred thousand pounds," said the voice.

"I haven't got it," I replied in a panic. "Be reasonable."

"Then you'll just have to find it. I am a reasonable man. I'll give you two weeks."

The line went dead.

After taking that call, I told myself that the man with the mechanical voice must be an accomplice of Jed Barker, someone I'd once met but had long since forgotten, and that the two of them had conspired together to blackmail me. And of course, I told myself that Jed had had it coming.

But in my heart of hearts, I knew the truth: I had killed the wrong man. Jed had had nothing to do with it. The blackmailer was someone else entirely.

Words cannot express the pain I felt when I realised that Jed had not been the culprit and I'd killed him unjustly.

To make matters worse, he'd tried to help me. He had done his best to conceal the evidence of my motive from the police. By some wicked irony, the evidence Jed had tried to suppress had only surfaced because I'd murdered him. Cause and effect. They can be such cruel masters, sometimes.

Every night since having the revelation that I killed an innocent man, I've been haunted in my dreams by the image of Jed, his head narrowed to a caricature of its former self by the grip of the vice, with his eyeballs slipping from their sockets like peeled nectarines from the grasp of an over-eager gourmand.

If you think you have any idea of the weight of guilt that I carry, think again.

No-one but the Damned can understand the grief of the Damned.

That grief, when it hit me, paralyzed me.

It made me incapable of dealing with pressure.

And I was under immense pressure:

- I had to find out who the blackmailer was, and eliminate him;
- I had to raise another £100,000 to keep him quiet until I succeeded in putting a stop to his grubby activities; and
- I had to find those bodies that Jim had hidden, so as to lay a false trail for the police.

I got confused and agitated. I didn't know which project to tackle first.

I was in such a tizz that I spent an entire day at my desk unable to come up with more than half a sentence.

Then I got upset with myself and determined to take action. I made a list – in my head of course – and prioritised what I had to do.

First, I visited a financial adviser and arranged a mortgage on Brian's flat. This gave me £100,000 in ready money to pay off the blackmailer. I hoped I wouldn't need it and that I'd be able to track him down and pay him in an altogether different currency. But I had the funds available, if the worst came to the worst.

Next I began to stake out Chu.

I reckoned that apart from Jed, he was the most

likely suspect. He'd given me the keys to Jim's house, so he must have had some idea of the equipment that Jim had in the cellar. It followed that he would have been able to work out who had used that equipment to carry out the Skull Crusher murders.

With Jim in prison, Chu would have thought, *it could only have been Brad Sharpe who had used a vice to kill the murder victims. Ergo, he must be the Skull Crusher.*

It wasn't long before my efforts paid off. I soon saw Chu driving through Chinatown, bold as brass, in a grey Ford Focus. Granted, the number plate was different to the one used by the blackmailer, but it stood to reason that he would have replaced the plates with legitimate ones after he'd fleeced me.

There had been a void in my life since Brian's death. I had felt it keenly.

Strange though it may seem, I needed someone in my life I could hate. Someone for whom I could work up a feeling of utter loathing. Brian had fulfilled that role admirably. He'd been an expert at being loathsome. He had given me all the material I needed to feel justified in totally detesting him.

With my traditional Hate Figure gone, I had no-one to detest.

Brian's death had created a vacancy.

Chu would fill it nicely.

I appointed him to his new post, and began to lay plans for his future, which, I suspected, would be decidedly short.

52

Putting paid to Chu would be difficult. I couldn't think how I would be able to get him to accept food or drink from me, laced with my favourite sedative. I decided I had no alternative other than to use a blunt instrument to stun him.

Then there was the problem of getting him out of his shop and into a car. How would I achieve that without being seen? People were on the lookout for men in flat caps and overalls these days, albeit younger men than me.

I wandered up and down the street where Chu had his medicine shop, and discovered that there was a narrow alley at the back. High walls divided the plots of land owned by every set of business premises from the plot owned by its neighbours. When Chu parked on his plot, which he did every day, he couldn't be seen by the people next door on either side.

This presented me with an opportunity.

I filled one of my old socks with gravel and experimented by banging it against a wall. It burst and the gravel flew everywhere. After much trial and error, I found that a four-sock thickness worked nicely to retain the gravel, even when I struck the wall with the hardest of blows.

Next, I practised in the bedroom when Sandra was out with the kids. I had an old mac that had rather large sleeves. I put my gravel weapon up the right sleeve and held it there by clenching my fist. I looked at myself in the mirror. It was impossible to tell I was armed in any way, especially when I stuck both hands in my pockets.

I practised opening my fist and letting the gravel-filled sock slide out of the sleeve into my hand by force of gravity. After that, I practised following that move up immediately with a vicious strike on a pillow. When I was able to let the weapon fall into my hand and deal the blow in one swift smooth action, I knew I was ready.

A few days later, I was walking through Chinatown in an old white mac with a grey trilby hat on my head. I caught a glimpse of myself in a shop window. I looked just like Sam Spade. That timeless image somehow gave me confidence.

When I knew there was no-one about, I darted into Chu's shop with my hands in my pockets. Chu seemed surprised.

"You again. What do you want this time?"

Hidden from his sight below the counter, my right hand was already opening and allowing the gravel-filled sock to slide from my sleeve into its grip.

"Well, you know that tonic you sold me?" I said. "I'd like another bottle, please."

Chu turned his back on me and reached out to the shelves behind him. As he did so, I leaned over the counter and the gravel-filled sock sliced through the air. It struck him on the back of the head with a dull thud. He turned and looked at me with an expression between pain and surprise, then slumped to the floor.

I locked the front door and changed the sign on it from "Open" to "Closed". Then I took his car keys and dragged him outside via the back door. With his car to the front of us, and high walls to either side of us, no-one could see me putting him into the boot – the boot of the car he had so recently used to part me from my money. I thought it fitting he should be carried to his doom in that same vehicle.

I drove to Palatine road. The coast was clear, so I entered the gates of the Old Chapel and closed them behind me. When I got out of the car, I heard birds chirping in the trees. I felt every bit as happy as they evidently did.

I loaded Chu onto the sack cart and got him downstairs into the chair in the cellar. Then I went back upstairs and enjoyed a brew while he came round. When I'd finished it, I returned to the cellar to interrogate him. Having recently been interrogated by the police myself, I felt I knew the ropes and was capable of doing a pretty good job of it.

Chu regained his senses with the aid of a bucket of ice-cold water thrown forcefully against his face.

"Hello Chu," I said.

"Where am I? What's going on?" He asked, with the icy water dripping from his hair and cheeks.

"I think you know," I told him. "But just in case you haven't worked it out yet, you're in Jim's cellar."

His eyes darted from side to side.

"Jim's cellar? What am I doing here?" He asked.

"I thought that would have been obvious. You're

helping me with my enquiries. It's a bit like when the police take someone in for questioning."

The expression on his face told me he didn't think it much resembled a trip to the local Nick.

"What enquiries?" He asked. Then he quickly added: "I'll tell you everything you need to know."

Co-operation; I liked that.

"Where is my money?" I asked.

He knitted his eyebrows.

"What money?"

I tightened up the vice to remind him.

"AAAAAAAAAAAAAAA!!! *that* money!" He said immediately. "It's in my shop!"

That was enough for me on that subject. I loosened the vice.

Then, at that moment, I froze.

I felt as if someone was watching me.

So conscious was I of the feeling of being watched, that I actually inspected the cellar floor to check whether Brian's missing eye was mouldering away somewhere in a dark corner, looking at me. I even searched beneath his discarded wig for it, sending a colony of beetles scuttling across the grimy floor to find alternative accommodation. But I could not detect any trace of an eye, so I continued with the task at hand.

"Where are the bodies?" I asked.

He looked pensive, then said:

"They're buried in my garden."

"You're a quick learner, Chu," I told him as I tightened the jaws for the final eye-popping time.

When the vice had done its work, I applied a razor to the top of his head and removed a large patch of his black hair, bringing new meaning to the expression "to have a close shave".

For good measure, I took a Stanley knife and scored a deep cross in his exposed scalp.

I peeled back his skin in four neat folds from the centre of the cross, to reveal the glistening bone beneath. Then I applied the brace and bit to the midpoint of the exposed square of bone, and began to turn the brace.

Chu made the usual squeals and pleas for mercy they all do. There is no point in describing that sort of thing again. You've heard it before. I have nothing new to add on the subject, and nor did Chu.

When I was done, I decided that the Skull Crusher would dispose of this body in a different way to the previous ones. It would be buried in a shallow grave in Speaker Woods. That would give them all something to think about. A change to the Skull Crusher's M.O.

I was in two minds about the disposal of the body. Part of me wanted it to be buried so well it would never be found; part of me wanted it to be quickly discovered, so that Brad Sharpe, fearless Crime Reporter, could resume writing about his favourite subject – the activities of his alter ego the Skull Crusher.

In the end, the part of me that wanted Chu to be discovered won out.

I made the grave very shallow indeed and left an abundance of clues that it *was* a grave. These included a naked foot sticking up like a signpost out of the soil.

I was certain that some passer-by going for a walk

in the woods would stumble across it, very soon, and report the matter to the police.

With Chu safely underground, I assumed I'd got rid of my Blackmailer, but events were to prove me wrong.

53

I got into Chu's shop without the need to commit the offence of breaking and entering, as I'd taken his keys. Once inside, I searched every square inch of it for my money, but failed to find anything of value, other than a small amount of shrapnel he'd left in the till.

Indignation welled up in my chest – he had lied to me.

Just after I'd left the shop by the rear entrance, I ran into Adkins in the narrow back street. I wondered whether he'd seen me making my exit.

"Mr Sharpe," he said courteously.

"Can I help you, D.I. Adkins?" I asked.

"No, I'm just taking a stroll, and looking for a restaurant to have my lunch in."

"What a coincidence, bumping into you here. Don't you work out of the Fallowfield station?"

He smiled.

"You might find a lot of coincidences happening from now on," he said. Then he came up close to me, and, still smiling, he hissed: "I know it's you Sharpe, and sooner or later I'm going to prove it."

My very brain spun like a top when I heard those words, but somehow I managed a bland smile. Then I shook my head, as if saddened by his misapprehension, and turned my back on him. As I walked away, I felt his eyes boring into my back.

When I was safely out of Adkin's sight, I went to my car and drove to Chu's house, being careful to ensure that I wasn't being followed.

When I got there, I found it didn't even have a garden.

I tried not to get too angry about it.

The days passed with no rumours down at the Nick about a new body being discovered. The days turned into weeks, and I began to wonder what was going on.

54

One night I was walking through a large cave. It was quite dark, but I could tell that the walls of the cave were white, like limestone. I felt them with my hands; they were smooth and damp.

As I neared the entrance to the cave, I saw more clearly what it was made of.

It was made of bone.

I was walking through Brian's eye socket.

I screamed out loud, then I realised that I'd been dreaming.

55

Waiting for Chu's body to be discovered proved to be more than I could bear. I worked myself up into a fine state of anxiety that was almost overwhelming.

I kept wondering whether the police knew something about it, and were keeping the information to themselves in order to get the better of me. I told myself that this was impossible, and that the cops always release details when a murder victim has been found. But still, I had the nagging feeling that on this occasion they were departing from the norm because they were setting a trap for me of some kind.

Another source of anxiety was the lack of good subject matter for my columns. I had nothing to write about, other than the usual shoplifting stories, and writing about them was boring and depressing. God alone knows what the readers must have made of it.

When I could stand the situation no longer, I decided to revisit Speaker woods and check Chu's grave to see whether anyone had come by and disturbed it.

I packed a spade in my car and headed for the

woods. When I got there, I drove near the site of the grave, parked in a convenient glade, and followed a winding path to the twisted tree I'd previously identified as a landmark.

While standing next to the tree, I looked around for the foot I'd left sticking up out of the ground, but I didn't see it. I supposed an animal may have eaten it, so I took the spade from the back of my car and began to dig a hole where I'd buried the body. Almost immediately, due to my lack of stamina, I became hot and breathless. Beads of sweat formed between my shoulder blades and trickled down my back.

I dug to a good depth but found nothing, so I moved to one side and dug another hole. Still nothing. By then I was perspiring freely, but I continued digging. I had to find out what was going on.

Within an hour there must have been at least half-a-dozen holes within close proximity of one another, each with a heap of damp black earth like a molehill next to it, but still I hadn't located the body of Chu. It was a living nightmare.

I returned to the first hole I'd dug, which was in the correct place, got on my hands and knees next to it, and began scraping away at the earth with my hands. Soon my fingers were scratched and bleeding. Apart from removing some skin from my fingertips, I achieved nothing.

So engrossed, had I become in my search, that I didn't notice the arrival of a young policeman. I looked up from my digging and saw him watching me.

"Hello sir," he said in a friendly way, "do you mind telling me what you're doing?"

Red in the face and panting from my labours, I gasped the words:

"Just give me a minute," and I stood up, and leant against my spade with my chest heaving.

My mind was turning more quickly than any electric fan, as I tried to think up plausible innocent reasons for being in the woods and digging a random series of holes.

"I'm looking for Medieval artefacts," I said at length. "I believe the Knights Templar had a settlement around here in about nine hundred A.D."

I prayed to God that the policeman wouldn't poke around in any of my holes and discover a body I had somehow overlooked.

"That's a rather unusual theory, if you don't mind me saying so, sir," he said.

He was one of the new pushy types that Bob Napper didn't much care for – the types who are keen to make names for themselves.

"I'm local to the area and something of an amateur historian myself," he continued, "and I've never heard of any Templar activity around here."

I tried to look as if I knew what I was talking about.

"There may be more Templar activity than you think, constable," I said.

He looked unconvinced.

"Is that your car over there, sir?" He asked, pointing between the trees.

I could not deny it.

"Yes, it's mine."

"Do you mind if I take a look in it?"

We walked together to the car. I was still breathing heavily, but by this time it was due to stress more than anything else. I was wondering what I had in the car that might be incriminating. Moreover, I worried that whether or not the constable found anything incriminating he might organise a search team to dig the area, and they would find Chu, and link me to his death.

Somewhat bizarrely, I wondered how my columns would report such a development. I couldn't stop myself. I didn't care to speculate about it, but against my will my mind began producing copy about my own exposure as the murderer:

"Bradley Sharpe, 59, former crime reporter on the Manchester Daily News, was yesterday revealed to be the psychotic killer behind the so-called "'Skull-Crusher' murders. Ironically, Sharpe has been the most vocal of the many commentators on the murders, and has regularly run campaigns calling for the public to help catch the killer. In the end, it was not the public response that led to his arrest, but good-old-fashioned police work. He was apprehended by a young policeman who found him involved in suspicious activity in Speaker Woods...."

The possibility that such a column might appear in the Manchester Daily News, of all places, forced me consider all of my options.

I soon realised I had only *one* option.

I unlocked the car for the constable and opened the tailgate; and he obligingly bent down and peered into the boot.

I'd believed I had crossed my Rubicon when I'd killed Brian but I had been mistaken.

The point at which I crossed my Rubicon occurred the instant that the young Constable looked into the boot of my car. Up until that moment, I had thought of myself as a normal man with a secret life as a serial killer. After that moment, I became a serial killer who spent most of his time masquerading as a normal man.

I swung the spade in an arc so the heavy end of it struck him on the back of the head. He was wearing a policeman's hard helmet, but it did him little good. He convulsed into a kneeling position at the rear of the car, like a supplicant at an altar. I bound his ankles and wrists, and somehow manoeuvred him into the back of the vehicle. Then I took him to my lair at the Old Chapel.

He woke up strapped to the chair in the darkling cellar.

"What's going on?" He asked.

It was the sort of question I had come to expect.

And you know the rest.

When I was done, I decided that I could not have another fiasco in which a body lay undiscovered, leaving me in a limbo wondering what was going on. I needed material for my columns; I needed to be *someone*; I needed to be needed, and yes, I needed the body to be found, just not found in a way that linked it to me.

I cleaned the cadaver thoroughly, and, on impulse, tied a length of rope around its neck that I'd found in one of Jim's cupboards.

After this one, I told myself, I would be free. I could retire from my life as the Skull Crusher.

If he would let me.

I drove out to the woods and left the body in an exposed position near a footpath.

Then I had second thoughts.

Taking the free end of the rope, I threw it so that it looped over the branch of a tree above my head, and pulled on it until the constable was hoisted so high that his feet left the ground; I tied the other end of the rope around the trunk of a smaller, neighbouring tree. The Constable hung there, twirling slowly around, like some grotesque banner proclaiming the triumphant return of the Skull Crusher.

It was a big risk going to such exhibitionist lengths. I could have been seen, or even caught in the nefarious act. But fortune smiled on me.

Within twenty-four hours I heard rumours that a policeman had been killed, and that the police were taking it very personally. It seemed I had stirred up a Hornet's nest of trouble for myself.

It made me wonder whether I'd done the right thing.

56

I t was about this time that I did something stupid that turned out, through no fault of my own, to be a brilliant masterstroke.

One day I parked on a back street to avoid the pay stations in Piccadilly and it was dark when I returned to my car. As I approached it, I noticed a young man watching me. He was wearing a Hoodie and a flat cap. As I extracted my car key from my pocket he advanced on me menacingly, took hold of the lapels of my suit jacket, and rammed me against the side of my car.

"Give me your wallet, Granddad," he hissed. "Now!"

A few months previously I would have meekly handed over the wallet and anything else he might have asked for. But I'd changed. I now had an alter ego who killed people. The Skull Crusher. He wasn't about to be scared into submission by a young punk like this.

I summoned up my strength and pushed him backwards. He was much younger than me, about thirty-five, but also much smaller. He may have only been five feet six or seven. I'm five-nine, and with my weight advantage (courtesy of my overlarge midriff) I was able to give him such a good shove that that he staggered. While he was busy regaining his balance, I threw a crude swinging right handed punch that caught him high up on the forehead. It must have hurt him, because it broke two of my knuckles.

He staggered again, and I went after him with my fists held high to defend myself. But at fifty-nine years old, and having taken no regular exercise more strenuous than having sex with Kimberly (which could be quite demanding in point of fact), I was already too tired to fight.

He leaped on me and grabbed me, and I fell backwards with my attacker on top of me. As I landed, the back of my head smacked against the pavement so hard that I heard it crack, and saw a flash of stars like a kaleidoscope being rotated in my brain, then I passed into a state of semi-consciousness.

Through the grey fog that enveloped me I was vaguely aware of my attacker's hands gripping my throat and squeezing. Then I heard someone shouting:

"Hey you, what the fucking hell do you think you're doing?"

I felt my attacker get off me and heard his footsteps recede into the distance.

My rescuer leant over me.

"Are you all right mate?" He asked.

I barely had the strength to reply.

"No," I gasped. "Please call an ambulance."

As soon as I'd uttered those words I passed out. I regained consciousness briefly in the ambulance then I lost it again.

The next thing I remember is opening my eyes to see Sandra and my police contact Bob Napper sitting next to me. I was in a hospital bed, and Sandra was holding my hand. There was an array of electronic equipment next to me monitoring my condition.

"Oh, darling," said Sandra, "you've woken up at last. How *do* you feel?"

I considered my answer. My head was pounding. I wiggled my fingers and toes. They seemed to be working.

"I'm okay," I told her. "I've got the mother of all headaches, that's all."

She smiled.

"Bob's here," she said. "He's here because he's worried about you. But he'd also like to ask you a few questions if you're up to it."

"I am. Fire away Bob," I said.

He looked grave.

"The bloke who did this to you, Brad, did you get a good look at him?" He asked.

"Very good," I told him.

"Do you have any idea who it was?"

I shook my head. I didn't shake it more than once because it hurt like hell.

"No idea," I said.

He put his hands on his knees and leaned forwards.

"The fellow who rescued you told us what happened. He was at the other end of the street when he saw this guy in a Hoodie and flat cap who seemed to be waiting for you. He could have been waiting for the first person coming alone into a deserted street, of course, to mug him, but we suspect he was waiting specifically for you. The man in the Hoodie attacked you, but you fought back. It looked as though he'd singled you out and tried to kill you. And we have a theory about that."

I wished I'd had my notebook. Without it I felt lost. It was like being without my memory. I determined to do my best to remember everything that Bob said that was remotely newsworthy.

"What's the theory, Bob?"

"The guy in the Hoodie who attacked you matches the criminal profile we have for the Skull Crusher. At least, that is, his height matches the likely height of the offender. What's more, he was wearing a Hoodie, and we have video evidence strongly suggesting the Skull Crusher sometimes wears a Hoodie. He also wore a flat cap. The Skull Crusher wears one of those, as far as we know. We think he uses the Hoodie and cap to hide his face from security cameras." (By this time even the Police were describing the killer as the Skull Crusher) "We think the man who attacked you could have been the Skull Crusher. It could be that you've made things difficult for him with your press coverage, and he wants you out of the way."

I tried not to look too happy about this turn of events.

"My goodness. I was lucky to get away with my life, then," I said.

"That could well be the case," Bob agreed. "He may have been planning to abduct you and give you the same treatment he gave the others. Luckily for you, there was a good Samaritan around who rescued you before it was too late."

I nodded. That hurt.

"Yes, I think I remember."

"What were you wearing when you were attacked?"

"I'm not sure. A shirt, maybe, and some kind of jacket."

"I'd like to borrow them," said Bob. "We'd like to have them tested. Your attacker's DNA could be on your clothes."

I hesitated, feigning a dizzy spell. I wasn't sure that I wanted my clothes testing for DNA. What if the police already had a DNA sample taken from one of the victims and it matched my own?

"I don't know where they are," I said, playing for time.

"In the cupboard next to your bed," said Sandra. "One of the nurses told me. The staff here are very helpful."

Aren't they just.

Bob took them.

"I'll bring you some more clothes when I visit this evening," said Sandra.

When I was well enough, I was asked to help put together a photofit picture of the man who had attacked me. To my eye, it looked uncannily like the Artist's impression of the Skull Crusher the MDN had commissioned only a short time before. It was soon being aired on all the news channels. It was also given a prominent position on the front page of the Manchester Daily News. There was a picture of me alongside it, sitting up in my hospital bed with a bandaged head and a bandaged right hand. I was grinning. I had every reason to.

The headline read:

"Brave MDN Reporter fights off Skull Crusher."

The breathless copy beneath it said something along the lines of:

"Manchester Daily News Crime Reporter Bradley Sharpe, aged 59, bravely fought off an attack by a man believed to be the Skull Crusher late last Friday night. The two of them were involved in a life and death struggle during which Mr Sharpe landed a punch on his assailant that staggered him, then they both fell to the ground grappling. David Jenner, a bystander who witnessed the attack, came to Mr Sharpe's aid and drove off the attacker. Mr Sharpe is currently in Manchester General Infirmary and his condition is said to be comfortable. He and Mr. Jenner have both helped police to compose a photo fit picture of the assailant. Now, for the first time, we can show you what the Skull Crusher may probably look like (see illustration, above). Etc."

The photofit was shown on Crimewatch, and police efforts were concentrated on finding the diminutive thirty-five year old who appeared to fit the profile.

I could breathe easily, other than for one minor glitch.

Adkins did not buy the "attacked by the Skull Crusher" story. He continued to obsess over the idea that the Skull Crusher might be me.

57

I n order to milk everything I could from my story about being attacked, I wrote a further story called *The Skull Crusher and Me* which recounted the episode, and analysed the many reasons that the Skull Crusher might have had for wanting to see me dead. Prime amongst these was probably the fact that I'd saved many potential victims by alerting them to the threat they faced, and advising them to take appropriate precautions every time they went out.

No wonder the Skull Crusher was so riled at me. I had denied him the easy pickings that he'd enjoyed at the beginning of his career.

In the wake of my heroics, the MDN received a deluge of emails and letters about the Skull Crusher. There was an editorial meeting to discuss how to make the most of the interest we were generating. Someone suggested a "Skull Crusher" themed competition. I think they were only half joking. Then someone else had the idea that since most of the correspondence was addressed to me, I should have a presence on a range of social websites to promote the Manchester Daily News.

Kimberly helped me put together a Facebook page and a weblog, both of which were linked to Twitter.

Within days I had an army of followers on Twitter and a similar army of Friends on Facebook.

I spent much of my work time, after that, Facebooking, Tweeting, and Blogging to my many new friends, followers, and admirers.

It was a hectic period in my life, but very rewarding.

My mail sack, real and virtual, constantly brimmed with positive correspondence about me. And in contrast with all the other newspapers in the country, the circulation of the Manchester Daily News was climbing relentlessly.

The increased circulation was something we bragged about to our advertisers, especially the ones who spent large sums of money with us. We brought our success to their attention (and guaranteed their loyalty) by paying for a box at Old Trafford to watch Manchester United in action, and plying them with food and drink during matches. (For those who were not United fans we also had a box at the City ground).

I was at one of these shindigs when we were entertaining the Directors of Manchester's most successful car dealership.

The second half of an exciting match had just started when a middle-aged woman with a sizeable tumbler of gin and tonic approached me. I realized it was Pat, the wife of Gerry, one of the Directors. I'd got to know him at some of the other corporate events we'd both attended – horse racing at Haydock, golf at Hopwood Park, that sort of thing.

"Hi," she said. "You're that reporter that everyone is talking about, aren't you?"

"Are they?" I asked. "It's news to me." (It wasn't, but I liked to assume an air of modesty, however false). "Anyway, you know what Oscar Wilde said. 'the only thing worse than being talked about is not being talked about.'"

She laughed. She must have been one of the few people I'd met who'd never heard that line before.

"I'm sure you know they are," she said. "You were so brave when that awful Skull Crusher thing attacked you. Anyway, you're obviously a very clever man. I want to ask your opinion on something."

A very clever man? Even I am susceptible to flattery, sometimes, and I felt rather pleased by the compliment.

"I don't know that I'm *that* clever," I protested. (Although I did). "Fire away."

"It's my fiftieth birthday this year," she said. "I'm thinking of asking Gerry for a facelift."

Pat was a good-looking woman. I say good-looking; her best days were clearly behind her. The bloom of youth was gone. But she hadn't completely lost her looks by any means.

Her age showed mainly in her face and throat. She had a fine figure and was still pretty, but her jawline was soft where once it had been firm, and her throat was beginning to show signs of becoming something that would one day resemble the neck of a Turkey.

"You what?" I asked, nearly spilling my pint. "Did I hear that right?"

"You did," she said. "I'm thinking of asking Gerry to buy me a facelift for my fiftieth birthday present."

"Why?" I asked.

She swirled her gin and tonic around in the glass and took a slurp that would have done justice to an alcoholic on his final bender.

"Well, I've given Gerry twenty good years now," she replied. "I've been an attractive wife for him all that time. But things are beginning to go, and I know it. And there's nothing I can do about it. I can exercise and diet to keep my figure, but I can't do anything about this." (She touched her face). "I sometimes see Gerry looking at other women, and I know why. They're younger than me. They look younger, and firmer, sexier."

"You don't think Gerry is going to cheat on you, do you?"

"No. But when he looks at other women, I know what he's thinking, and I know what he wants. He doesn't want an old bag like me. I want to give him what he wants. I'm okay from the neck down but from the neck up I'm not a young woman any more. That's why I want a facelift. What do you think Gerry will say if I ask him for one?"

I felt under considerable pressure when faced with this question. I answered it as diplomatically as I could.

"Well, I'm sure Gerry wants to make you happy. But he probably likes you just the way you are, and he won't want you to have an operation unless it's for sound medical reasons. So he won't want you to have a facelift. He'll be worried about the risk to your health. But if he thinks you want it really badly, he might go along with it just to please you. All that any married man wants to do at the end of the day is to make his wife happy."

JACK D MCLEAN

She nudged me with her elbow.

"What's your secret anyway?" She asked.

"What do you mean?"

"Well, I don't mean to be rude, but you're obviously not young, and yet you – you – you *seem* young, somehow. How do you do it?"

"If that's true, it's because I have a young attitude. I'm young at heart."

And I've disposed of a few people who were beginning to annoy me. That no doubt helps, I thought.

She drained the last of her gin and tonic and staggered out to the toilets.

I was left to reflect on the interesting effects of fame and murder.

Fame had made me into nothing less than an Oracle, and my homicidal exploits had turned back the clock on my ageing process, made me seem young, and even – I dared say – attractive, to the opposite sex.

Later, I overheard one of our Directors talking to a guest.

"We sometimes invite minor celebrities to lend a bit of glamour to the proceedings," he said. "We've had Mick Hucknall's manager here before now. Tonight though, we have our very own Bradley Sharpe."

This was an interesting development. Apparently I was now classed as a *Minor celebrity,* on a par with Mick Hucknall's manager. *Minor celebrity.* I repeated the words several times in my head: *minor celebrity, minor celebrity.*

This raised an interesting question: would I be promoted by subsequent developments in the life of the Skull Crusher to the ranks of the C-List Celebs, or even higher? B-list, or (and I hardly dared hope for this) A-list?

Whether I'd be promoted or not, I was determined to milk every last bit of enjoyment I could from being any sort of a celebrity.

When I got home, Sandra was still up, messing about on the Internet. I was bursting to tell her my news about being regarded as a *minor celebrity*.

"Who's this Kimberly Jones then?" She enquired as I walked into the study.

My happy thoughts about celebrity departed in an instant.

My legs went weak with panic.

Just how much did she know?

58

"She's a work colleague," I said, with as steady a voice as I could muster. "I've mentioned her before. Why do you ask?"

"She's rather attractive, isn't she?"

"I suppose she is," I agreed, in a manner that suggested I hadn't noticed, and wasn't at all interested in that sort of thing. "Anyway, how do you know about her?" (What I really meant was, *what exactly do you know about the two of us?*)

"She's one of your Facebook friends," she said.

I breathed a sigh of relief.

Sandra, being so much younger than me, had been on Facebook for as long as I could remember, and she knew all about the wretched thing. Anyway, thankfully, having Kimberly as a Facebook friend didn't seem to arouse her suspicions.

Although it should have.

My activities on social websites soon brought me a number of Trolls who were out to undermine my activities, and a much larger number of campaigning followers who devoted their time to undermining the activities of the Trolls.

At length, a strange thing happened. I received a Facebook "Friend Request" from someone calling himself "Skull Crusher". Out of curiosity, I accepted his request. Then I realised that it might be something that would help the police with their enquiries, so I told them about it, and they put their techies on the job of locating the I.P. address of my sinister new Facebook friend.

Shortly afterwards, I had a friend request from someone calling himself "The Manchester Skull Crusher". Again, I accepted the request and informed the police.

Before long, I was friends with over a dozen people, all of whom used different variations of the words "Skull Crusher" in their names. I forwarded all the information to the police, who had more suspects and more lines of enquiry than they could possibly have known what to do with.

This led me to reflect that things were going swimmingly in some areas of my life.

Unfortunately, whenever that happens, there is always someone who comes along and spoils it for you. In my case, it was Mike Rudd, the Associate Editor who thought he was twenty years younger than his chronological age, in spite of the mountain of evidence that he wasn't.

Rudd somehow found out, or worked out, that I had become rather close to Kimberly.

59

He buttonholed me one day by the water cooler.
"What's going on with you and Kim then?"
He asked.

I looked suitably aghast.

"Whatever do you mean?" I replied. "We're work colleagues, nothing more. And by the way, her name is Kimberely."

He nudged me in the ribs with his elbow. I have always found being nudged in the ribs by someone's elbow particularly annoying.

"Come off it," he said. "I've seen the way you're always hanging around with her. There's more to it than that."

I groped for a response to put him off the scent.

"Well," I answered, "you might think so, but we don't all cheat on our wives, you know."

Rudd rolled his eyes.

"It's not like that, Brad, and you know it. I've been unhappy in my marriage for years. I always told Pearl I'd leave her as soon as the kids were old enough. Let's have a drink so I can explain it to you."

The prospect of another drink with Rudd was

about as welcome as a mug of Hemlock. However, I didn't want him bleating whatever he knew or suspected about me and Kimberly to all and sundry, so I agreed to meet up with him after work. As it was Friday, that meant taking him out round the pubs in the Northern Quarter with my drinking buddies.

I didn't doubt that he would find a way to bore me rigid, but at least there would be others present to share the burden.

We met in The Castle Hotel. My friends Jez and Baz were already there. I greeted them and explained that Rudd would be joining us.

"Not that wanker," said Baz. "He's right up himself. And if he thinks I'm going to any more puffy wine bars, he can think again."

"Too right," said Jez. "I was gagging for decent a pint all night last time he came out with us, and dragged us into those shit-holes he calls bars."

"Don't worry," I told them. "We'll have a gentleman's agreement between us not to let him talk us into anything rash this time."

There was a band setting up in a corner. The lead singer was the famous rock star Liam Gallagher, who was making a surprise appearance at the pub in an effort to get back to his roots. He recognised me and came over and had a chat. After he left, I bemoaned the pressures of celebrity to Baz and Jez, but I doubted that they understood what I was going through.

A few minutes later, Rudd arrived to ruin things. I immediately downed my drink and prepared myself for the onslaught of self-justifying claptrap that was sure to come from Rudd, once he'd got into his stride.

After two or three pints, he turned to me, and said:

"You see, I was very young when I married Pearl, and I only married her because she was pregnant and bzzz bzzz bzzz bzzz and you know bzzz."

Then Jez said:

"I'm going out for some fresh bzzz."

And very soon the conversation sounded like this:

Rudd: "So I had no alternative other than bzzz bzzz bzzz and let her have the house bzzz bzzz savings bzzz bzzz bzzz living with Monica now bzzz but money tight bzzz bzzz greedy cow got her hands on half the pension bzzz bzzz bzzz."

Baz: "Is bzzz ready for a bzzz bzzz?"

Jez: "Mine's a bzzz of bzzz"

Rudd: "Bzzz bzzz bzzz"

Jez: "Bzzz, bzzz bzzz bzzz!"

Baz: "Bzzz?"

I wondered what could be happening. Then I realised what it was.

Important folk like me should not associate with insignificant people like Baz, Jez and Rudd, I thought. They are insects. I have outgrown them all.

During this period there was a lull in the work of Manchester's most notorious (indeed only) serial killer, so I had more spare time on my hands than usual. I busied myself by fulfilling a long-held ambition. I wrote a true-crime book along the lines of "In Cold Blood", by Truman Capote. It was called *The Skull Crusher Murders,* and the inside flap of the dust cover assured readers that it provided the hidden story behind the headlines.

This was a lie, of course. It did nothing of the sort.

It is only now that I am giving you the hidden story.

What the book did do was provide readers with a greater insight into the murders than my columns in the Manchester Daily News had done.

I achieved an "astonishing immediacy" with my prose (according to the Bolton News), and conveyed "all the true horror of the crimes" (according to a review in The Cheshire and North Western Express).

I wrote the book in the first person, Gonzo style, and told readers how I spent my days working for an important regional newspaper, and how I'd helped shape the headlines that had stunned the world.

By this time, more information about the M.O. of the Skull Crusher Murderer had entered the public domain, and I was able to speculate freely on such matters as the sound that a victim's skull might have made, as it finally gave way under the pressure of the vice ("a sort of soggy crunching noise like the splintering of wood taken from a dead tree.").

This was, as you now know, more than mere speculation.

I used the book to pose the question that was on everybody's lips: what kind of an individual could commit such atrocities? (My answer: He would be "pitiless and quite without remorse"; "a callous Monster"; "wicked beyond belief"; "Devoid of all human feeling, the Psychopath's Psychopath"; and so on).

Part of me balked at writing such things, as I knew them to be gross distortions of the truth, and I felt uneasy about sacrificing my journalistic integrity on the altar of sensationalism. But I salved my conscience by telling myself that this was a view that deserved to be explored, as much as the theory I believed to be the correct one, namely: that the Skull Crusher was a hugely talented but otherwise ordinary man, who had been driven by events to perform extraordinary acts he would not have so much as considered, had circumstances been different. (The editor of my book, by the way, prevailed on me to omit this theory from the final text, on the grounds that it wouldn't go down at all well with the reading public).

Comparisons are always odious, but it must be observed that *The Skull Crusher Murders* far outsold my brother's book *Living with Demons*, in spite of the massive advantage he enjoyed by being a dead author who had published his works posthumously. What is more, my Agent sold the film rights to *The Skull Crusher Murders,* and there is currently a major movie in the pipeline. (The cover of my book informed readers about this development: in the bottom right hand corner the words "soon to be a major movie" were tastefully emblazoned in white letters against a bright red background).

In contrast, *Living with Demons* has not received any interest from movie moguls, and likely never will.

With (as I fondly thought at the time) my Blackmailer dead, there was no need for me to carry out any more murders, and I believed I might have exhausted whatever reservoir of emotion had driven me to commit murder in the first place.

But rather worryingly, when one person or another upset me, I would look at him and say to myself: *I wonder what he would look like in a vice. It might rather suit him. At any rate, it would certainly be an improvement.*

This thought informed me that the Skull Crusher had not gone away for good, but was merely dormant for the time being. Like many a volcano, he would sooner or later erupt.

I laid plans for what I should do if the need to become the Skull Crusher became strong enough to overpower my restraint. I decided that I'd take prisoners who had served their terms, and use them as sacrificial lambs. I persuaded myself that this would not be a crime; it would be more like a service to society. After all, the statistics proved that they were likely to offend again, causing untold distress to their victims.

The urge couldn't be satisfied simply by purging annoying people from my life. It would be folly to do that.

It would bring the authorities down on me like a sack of bricks thrown from a cart, and that would never do.

Apart from these inner conflicts, life was normal, and normality was welcome after the many months of stress I'd experienced during the terrifying reign of the Skull Crusher. Normality had a glow it had lacked before. There were many reasons for this: I was on better terms with Sandra than I had been previously; I was still experiencing a renewal of my youthful vigour (indeed, Kimberley often remarked on how much energy I had for a man of my age); and I'd become a celebrity of sorts.

Of course, in some ways life could never be normal again. I harboured a terrible secret and however much I strived to suppress it, my secret would haunt me for the rest of my days. It often filled my head with distressing images as I slept. Sometimes I experienced flashbacks when I was wide-awake. I cannot say they were always unwelcome.

61

M ost aspects of my life were going well, but there were two things that continued to perplex me. One was the knowledge that Adkins was still digging away at the facts, trying to pin the murders on me. It seemed that every time I turned a corner he was waiting for me, observing my movements. It had a most unsettling effect on my nerves.

The other was the disappearance of Chu's body.

I told myself that I must have forgotten where I'd buried it, but this explanation never quite convinced me.

After a while, I accepted that I could do nothing about resolving the issue of the missing body, other than fret about it occasionally.

But as far as Adkins was concerned, there was one measure I could take.

I could resume my efforts to find the remains of Jim Kennedy's victims.

If I did that, and removed all traces of Jim's DNA from them, and somehow got news of my discoveries out after Jim had died, it would surely prove beyond doubt (or at least prove to the satisfaction of the police) that I had not committed any of the murders.

This was my logic:

All the murders had the same MO, or one that was to all intents and purposes the same, and this would strongly suggest they had all been committed by the same murderer.

There would be no link between me, and most of the victims.

Ergo, I couldn't be the killer.

D.I. Adkins would be discredited once and for all.

My scheme would get me off the hook, and, at the very least, it would throw a considerable spanner in the workings of their investigation.

So I redoubled my efforts to locate the bodies of Jim's victims.

Little did I know that this quest, which I thought would lead to my deliverance, would in fact precipitate my downfall.

62

A day or two after my night out with Rudd, I received a telephone call from a woman who had a refined voice and sounded young and attractive.

"Is that Mr Sharpe?" she asked.

"That's me," I confirmed. "How can I help?"

"I'm calling from the television show *Walker's Weekly*. You might have heard of it."

Walker's weekly was a chat show hosted by Gordon Walker, a burly former soap-star who'd left the soap in which he'd made his name, and branched out into other areas of television.

"I have," I confirmed. "I've even watched it once or twice. It's a good show."

"I'm pleased to hear you think that, Mr. Sharpe. My name is Zabida Hussain, and I'm a researcher for the show. I'm calling to tell you the good news that Gordon has personally asked if you'll agree to appear on *Walker's Weekly*. I hope you'll accept the invitation. It'll do wonders for your profile."

I saw at once that an appearance on the show could promote me into the heady realms of C-list, or even B-list celebrity status, so I didn't have to think about my answer.

"I'd love to come on the show. Wait a minute, will I be allowed to mention my book and film?"

"Of course you will. Gordon and his producers want you on the show *because* of your book and film."

"Brilliant. What are the arrangements?"

She gave me the details and told me everything would be confirmed by email. She said I could bring two guests to sit in the audience if I wanted, and that if I brought my wife along, she'd be allowed into the hospitality room with me.

I wondered if the show it might be a stepping-stone to bigger things such as *I'm a Celebrity Get me Out of Here,* or *Celebrity Big Brother,* or some similar reality TV program.

"Sandra," I said as soon as she walked through the door. "Guess what! I'm going to be on television! I've been invited to appear on Walker's Weekly. I'm going to be interviewed by Gordon Walker himself!"

"That's fantastic news, Brad. Will I be allowed to be in the studio audience?"

I could hardly contain myself.

"Better than that. You'll be allowed in the hospitality room with me before the show. We'll both be able to mingle with the other guests. I wonder who we'll meet."

63

The MCTV (Manchester Community Television) studio, from which Walker's Weekly was broadcast live (almost; there was a five-minute delay to allow for gaffes etc.), was housed in a large shed, on an industrial estate near Salford's prestigious Media City.

Sandra and I pulled into the car park at about 9.00 p.m., two hours before the show was due to air. As I pulled up, I noticed a car drive slowly past the entrance of the studio car park.

Instinctively I knew what was going on.

"Someone's been following us," I told Sandra. "I'm going to see who it is."

She put her hand on my wrist.

"Brad, please don't do that. It might be the Skull Crusher again."

I opened the door of the car.

"Don't worry, I can handle myself," I told her. "Just remember, I gave him something to think about last time he attacked me. He's not going to be in a hurry to try it again."

"Please be careful. I don't want to lose you, Brad."

"You won't lose me, Sandra," I assured her. "I'm not frightened of the Skull Crusher. I've met him before, and I reckon I've got his measure."

She turned pale but she didn't try to dissuade me again.

I left the car park, walked to the car that had been following us, and knocked on the window. The driver wound it down. He was, as I expected, D.I. Adkins.

"Well, D.I. Adkins, fancy meeting you here," I said. "What are you up to?"

"I'm just taking a late drive," He replied.

I bent down so that my face filled his field of vision.

"I don't think so. This looks very much like the harassment of a law-abiding citizen to me. I might have to report you to your superiors and to the Police Complaints Commission."

A shadow crossed his face, but he quickly recovered his poise.

"Do your worst," he said." I'm very familiar with the law on harassment, and I've been very careful to stay just on the right side of it."

At that moment I had an idea.

"Look, D.I. Adkins, I don't see why there should be any ill-will between us," I told him. "I'd like to mend fences. There's no point in you sitting outside in the cold. If you want to keep an eye on me, why don't you come in and watch the show? I've got a free ticket going spare."

"The show?" He asked.

He must have been the only person in the entire Greater Manchester area who had somehow failed to register the fact that I was due to appear on television that night.

"I'm going to be on Walker's Weekly. Surely you know of it?"

He didn't, but he agreed to join the studio audience.

Approximately two hours later, I was introduced live on air by Gordon Walker (or GW as he liked to be known), the genial shaven-headed host of Walker's Weekly.

"Mr Sharpe," he said. "I believe that your very beautiful wife is with us today."

"She is," I said. "She's in the front row over there."

The camera zoomed in on Sandra and she smiled, and did a little wave. She looked stunning. Next to her, Adkins sat stony-faced.

"You must know what I'm going to ask you first, Brad. What does it feel like to be attacked by the Skull Crusher?"

"In a word, *scary*."

"Take us through it, step by step. What happened exactly?"

"Picture the scene. I went to my car, which I'd parked on a back street. There was no-one around. Then, this figure appeared out of nowhere. He was wearing a Hoodie and a flat cap.

He got hold of me and rammed me up against my car. I pushed him away then swung a punch at him, and caught him on his forehead.

He was stunned. He staggered and I went on the attack. We struggled. Then I tripped up on something, fell backwards, and he landed on top of me. He put his hands around my throat and started to squeeze the life out of me. Luckily there was a Good Samaritan who chased my attacker away. I was injured, but I've made a full recovery."

"Have the police any theories about who the Skull Crusher might be, Brad?"

"Plenty, including a rather novel one."

"I'd like you to help me explain it, GW, if you don't mind, by putting a camera on the front row of the audience."

A camera duly panned in that direction.

"That's good," I said. "Thank you. There's a bald man in spectacles sitting next to my wife. Please focus on him."

The face of D.I. Adkins filled a wall-sized screen that acted as a backdrop to GW and me. I pointed at Adkins.

"That man is Detective Inspector Adkins of the Greater Manchester Police," I announced. "He believes that the Skull Crusher and me are one and the same person."

A silence fell over the entire auditorium. Then someone began laughing. After a second or two, everyone was laughing out loud, including GW.

This was *Television*.

More; it was *Theatre*.

Adkins looked furious. He turned bright red right from his shirt collar to the top of his bald pate. Then he stood up and stomped out of the studio.

My appearance on the show was favourably reviewed in the Manchester Daily News, which gave over a half-page to the event, and included a photograph of GW and me together. We looked so comfortable in one another's company that we were accused in some sectors of the media of having begun a "Bromance."

64

That was the high point of my career as a crime reporter, serial killer, and celebrity.
But what of the low point?
Please be patient. I am coming to that.

65

Two days after my appearance on Walker's Weekly I received a telephone call from Bob Napper.

"Brad," he said. "We've received the results of the DNA tests on the clothes you wore when you were attacked."

I began to feel queasy.

"Oh yes," I said.

"Unfortunately they've drawn a blank. Sorry, Brad. I wish I had better news for you, something that would help your brother, and your friend Jed. Well, you know what I mean, as far as they can be helped."

"That's all right Bob," I told him. "You did your best."

"Oh, and Brad," he said.

"Yes Bob?"

"Nice work on that show. I've never liked Adkins."

We both chuckled.

"Thanks Bob. See you."

"See you."

Elated by the news, I left the office with a distinct spring in my step.

As I made my way across the car park, Adkins descended on me, seemingly out of nowhere. He was looking well pissed off. He had his assistant Blake in tow.

"Mr Sharpe," he said. "Would you please accompany us to the station to take part in an identity parade?"

I didn't need to be told what that meant. It meant that the man who had helped me to load up Jed Barker into the boot of Barker's own car had come forward, and been asked to identify the Man in the Flat Cap.

I nearly wet myself at the prospect of appearing in a line-up with him on the other side of a one-way mirror. But what choice did I have? If I refused, it would appear suspicious, and Adkins could, in any event, use some legal power to compel me to appear before his witness. So with a heavy heart I agreed.

Adkins and Blake took me to the station and I was led into a large grey windowless room full of men of various ages and heights. There was a table in the middle of the floor that had a pile of overalls and flat caps on it.

A bored-looking middle-aged constable looked at me and selected a pair of overalls from the pile.

"Please put these on, sir." I did as I was asked. He handed me a flat cap. "Now please put this on."

Soon, all the men in the room other than for the two policemen who were present were clad in overalls and flat caps.

Adkins made an announcement.

"Gentlemen, please go to that side of the room," he said, pointing to one of the long walls.

We all shuffled to the wall.

"Please form a line facing the mirror on the other side of the room," Adkins added.

We stood there unmoving, looking at ourselves in the mirror for about a minute.

"Please all turn to face right."

We faced right.

"Please turn to face left."

We faced left.

"You and you and you, please step forward."

I was one of the people asked to step forward.

"You," (he pointed at me), "I'd like you to say: 'thank you, you've been a big help.'"

"Thank you," I said, in my most extreme Mancunian accent. "You've been a big help."

He pointed at the second person chosen from the line-up, a man of a similar age and height to me.

"Now you," he said.

"Thank you, you've been a big help," said the man, in lilting Irish tones.

A second or two later, another policeman entered the room and whispered in Adkins' ear.

The man with the Irish accent was invited to hang around for questioning, and the rest of us were told we could leave.

I made my exit with a bit of a smirk on my face. Adkins ran after me and caught up with me just before I escaped.

"Hubris is often followed by Nemesis, Mr. Sharpe," he said.

"You're whistling in the dark, Adkins," I replied, skipping happily out the front door.

It had been a good result for me, but at the same time it convinced me that I would never be safe as long as Adkins was sniffing around the evidence. This made it more urgent than ever that I should find Jim's cache of buried bodies.

I read again the few words he'd written about the way that he disposed of them:

"Later I took Simon through the tunnel and laid him to rest in the catacombs."

Where were the catacombs?

I went to the Manchester Library, a resource housed in a fabulous building in St Peter's Square and bearing a passing resemblance to the Pantheon. Once inside, I delved into the reference section in search of clues, perusing local maps, ancient and modern, archived newspapers, and history books. Eventually I discovered the patch of land beneath the Old Chapel on Palatine Road had been used as a cemetery since medieval times. Moreover, it had once been owned by the Knights Templar, a sect known for their spectacular underground architecture.

Was it possible, I wondered, that the Old Chapel was built on top of the catacombs to which Jim had referred in his journal, and that I had only to look in the right place, or in the right way, to find them?

I was unable to visit the Old Chapel during the day to find out as I'd spent half of the day in the library. I had to spend the remaining half making up for lost time by writing copy for my newspaper columns.

At the end of the working day I went home and saw to the kids. I was getting on better than ever with Sandra, and it pained me to lie to her, and tell her I had to meet a business contact about a story. But lie to

271

her I did. Then I drove to the Old Chapel equipped with a rucksack containing a miner's lamp and the other items I'd need to explore the catacombs – if, that is, I was able to find them.

I donned my gear and descended to the cellar. Under the baleful light provided by the single naked bulb, I tapped on all the walls. They seemed to be solid enough. Then I examined every square foot of floor space in search of a trapdoor, but there was none. I even tried to move the wooden cabinet to one side to see if there was a trapdoor beneath it, or a door concealed behind it, but it wouldn't budge. I inspected it more carefully. It seemed to have been built into the wall, or bolted to it in some way.

I opened the doors of the cupboard and looked inside. I had to turn on my miner's lamp to get a good view of the interior.

There were half a dozen shelves in it with pickle jars on them, and nothing more.

I removed one of the pickle jars and held it up to the light to examine the pickles it contained. It resembled a cauliflower.

In a moment I realised that it wasn't cauliflower; it was pieces of brain tissue floating in some kind of clear preservative. I dropped the jar in horror, and it smashed on the stone floor into a thousand pieces. Shards of glass, liquid, and blobs of brain flew in all directions.

It made me wonder if I needed to find the bodies. Would a number of pickle jars transported to a suitable location be enough to throw Adkins off my scent?

Perhaps, but how much more convincing would a

body be? I wondered. And, come to that, how much more convincing would a number of bodies be?

The lowest shelf in the cupboard was positioned about three feet above the floor. I got on my hands and knees and inspected the dark wooden panel beneath the shelf. I tapped it; it sounded hollow. My pulse quickened.

Could it be? I asked myself. *Could it really be?*

The panel looked nailed into place rather clumsily. Two rusting nails stuck out from awkward angles.

I took them between my fingers and thumbs and pulled at them, and the panel slid forward to open on concealed hinges.

At the back of it was a tunnel no more than three feet high and three feet wide. How long it was I could not tell. When I shone my torch into it, the beam failed to penetrate the deep gloom to its end.

Dare I enter?

I felt I had no choice. I had to find out if I was right about the bodies.

66

I got on my hands and knees and began to crawl through the dark confined space. It was stiflingly claustrophobic and so low I had to remove my rucksack and push it before me, obscuring my view of what lay ahead. It made progress difficult.

It also gave me a revelation.

The reason for the extra wheels on Jim's sack cart was to enable him to push it while it was lying flat on the ground with a body on it, just as I was pushing my rucksack.

I emerged from the tunnel onto a stone floor with headroom enough for me to stand. Before me, a spiral staircase descended into the darkness.

I took a deep breath, summoned up my courage, and descended the staircase.

At the bottom, I found myself in a long corridor with a vaulted stone ceiling. Other corridors connected to it at right angles, and there were fantastical carvings in the stonework.

After tying my ball of string to a carving of a devil at the bottom of the spiral staircase, I set off down the darkling corridor, trailing the length of string behind me.

When I came to the first turning in the corridor, I lit a candle and set it on the floor before continuing my journey, unravelling my ball of string as I proceeded.

I took several more turnings, all the while confident that my string and candles would take me safely back to my starting point.

After a while, I noticed that the string seemed to have become somewhat slack. I retraced my steps, following the line of string back to the last corner that I had turned.

The string went no further than to that last corner. Just around it, the end of the string was lying on the stone floor. It had been cut cleanly through with a sharp knife or a pair of scissors.

Panic gripped me.

There is someone else down here, I thought. *What kind of a person is he? What if he is some kind of a psychopath?*

I took a few moments trying and failing to get my bearings, then, as best I could, began heading back to the spiral staircase.

After a while, I realised what I should have known as soon as I'd discovered that my string had been cut: I was hopelessly lost. All I could do was to wander around randomly, and hope that chance would take me to the staircase.

I entered a circular vaulted chamber. All around it were man-sized alcoves set in the curved wall, each containing a man standing upright, staring at me with an expression of pain and suffering on his grey face.

For a moment I had palpitations, but when I

realised these were dead men, my fear subsided, though not by much. I had stumbled on Jim's catacombs, for what good it would do me now.

I walked around the chamber examining each cadaver in turn. They were perfectly preserved, perhaps by some ancient and long-forgotten Templar technology.

Before I'd done the rounds of all of them, I shone my torch on the face of one and felt dread claw at my stomach. I knew him.

It was Chu.

But that was impossible.

I'd buried him in Speaker Woods.

My knees felt as if they were going to collapse under my own weight, but somehow they continued to support me.

Up ahead of me, one of the victims emerged from its resting place in the alcove, turned, and walked rapidly towards me.

I became rooted to the spot. That is an expression I've heard many times in my life, and until that day I had never really known what it meant. It was clear enough to me that night what it meant: it meant that I could not move a muscle, even though every fibre of my being was telling me to turn and flee as fast as I possibly could.

The thing advanced upon me, and before I could react, it struck me a terrible blow on the top of my head.

I fell like a sack of wet sand hurled from the back of a moving truck, but I must have been conscious, because I felt my head crash painfully against the stone floor.

In a state of semi-consciousness, I was aware of being dragged by my feet.

The next thing I remember was being strapped to some piece of apparatus or other.

A stretcher. Yes, that is it, a stretcher, I thought, and almost cried out in relief.

I was horizontal and being pushed on a wheeled stretcher through a long narrow tunnel. *It must be the ambulance men,* I surmised. *They've been called, and they've come to take me to hospital to receive treatment for the bump on my head.*

Then an awful revelation hit me: it wasn't a stretcher. It was a sack cart. A specially modified sack cart for transporting bodies around in the Old Chapel.

And I lost consciousness.

I came to my senses, in pitch blackness, with a pounding headache.

Somehow, even though I could see nothing, I could tell I was in a sitting position.

I tried to move my arms and legs, but something was holding them fast. Then I tried to look around, but I couldn't turn my head.

I wondered if I might have died and gone to Hell.

I do not know how long I sat there in the darkness. It could have been minutes or hours, or even days, as I slipped in and out of consciousness. But eventually I opened my eyes and was able to see my surroundings. They were illuminated by a single naked bulb.

My arms and legs were firmly secured to the wooden chair in Jim's cellar. No wonder I'd been unable to move them. And as for my head, it was trapped in the vice. Fortunately, the vice had not been tightened to the point of pain, only to the point where I was immobilised.

When I realised what my circumstances were, I felt an emotion that was beyond fear and beyond even panic, and I screamed fit to bring the place down. But no-one could hear me. No-one, that is, except for my captor.

My screaming was interrupted by a familiar voice to one side of me. It was trying to provide me with a few crumbs of comfort. It did not succeed.

"There, there," said the voice. "There's no need for all that. There's nothing to be frightened of. "

And Jim Kennedy stepped into view.

"Jim," I said. For an instant I didn't know whether to feel relief or dread. Then I decided on dread. "What are you doing here?"

"I got my early release on compassionate grounds after all. I appealed a second time and my appeal was successful."

"But you were dying. You were so bad that you were taken into the prison hospital. I wanted to visit you, but I wasn't allowed to see you."

He smiled the sly smile that I recalled from our first meeting.

"My condition didn't deteriorate, I was faking it. I thought it might help with my appeal, and I was right. I managed to convince the doctors that I had only days to live, or weeks at the most. That clinched it for me. I was allowed out on compassionate grounds. Oh, by the way, I liked your letter. It was so nice that I've kept it. Look."

He withdrew a tatty folded piece of paper from one of his pockets, unfolded it, and held it before my eyes. It was indeed the letter I'd sent him when he'd been staying in the prison hospital.

They say that the best thing to do in a hostage situation is to engage your captors and try to talk to them, so that they see you as a human being rather than just an object to be disposed of at will. I decided to try it.

"Thank God you're still alive, Jim. It's good to see you. What have you been up to?" I asked.

His brow furrowed.

"To be honest, I haven't been behaving myself, Brad. I've been let out of prison on a licence, and I've breached the terms of it several times."

I tried to appear interested in his licence rather than in the only thing that was occupying my thoughts – my escape from his clutches.

"How's that, Jim? What have you done?"

I shuddered to think, but I had to ask.

"Well, for starters there's the blackmail," he said.

Cogs began to turn in my mind rather rapidly.

"You mean it was you who was blackmailing me?" I asked.

He smiled slyly once again.

"I'm afraid it was.".

"Why?" The obvious question, indeed, the only question.

"Because I hadn't enough money to continue with my work. I'm dying, as you know, and I wanted to make sure that I could do the things I need to do before I finally go. There are a great many things I have to do, Brad, to help mankind. I originally thought I might need as much as £200,000 to complete my mission. But I came to realise that the £100,000 you kindly gave me would be enough.""

I clutched at straws.

"I know your secret, Jim, I know you're the Angel Gabriel, the Strong Man of God." I said. "I can provide you and God with more of a tribute than I've already given you. Just tell me how much you want and I'll get it for you."

He shook his head.

"That won't be necessary. I now have all the money I need for the remaining period of my mortal life here on Earth."

"I can help you," I pleaded. "I can help with your legacy, Jim. You want a legacy, don't you? Just set me free, and I'll give you one. I can guarantee you a double page spread in the Manchester Daily News all to yourself. I might even be able to swing a pull-out colour supplement all about you, if you just give me the chance."

He seemed to brighten up a little.

"You may have something there. I'll get you a microphone and a tape recorder. You can dictate your thoughts into it for the entire week that your purification will last. You can record all that you know that could secure my legacy. After you've gone, I'll have the tape recording of your words typed up and sent to the newspapers."

I shuddered.

"After I've *gone*?" I gasped. "Where will I be going?"

"There is a space for you in the Catacombs," he said. "Perhaps you noticed it."

Then he left.

I tried as hard as I could to get free, but it was no use.

Jim returned a few hours later. He pulled the

table up close to me, set a tape recorder on it, and attached a microphone. He put the microphone on a flexible stand and placed it near to my mouth.

"Try that," he said.

It was in the perfect position for me to dictate to, but I was in no mood to dictate so much as a single sentence.

"I can't. I'm too thirsty to speak," I croaked.

I'd been without food and water for several hours, maybe for days. Jim produced a bottle with a straw in it and held the straw up to my lips.

"Drink this," he said.

I sucked the contents into my parched mouth.

"What is it?" I asked.

"Holy water, blessed by a priest," he told me.

"I'm hungry," I wailed. "Please can I have some food? Even if it's only a Big Mac or something?"

"I'm afraid not Brad," he replied. "It's just holy water for you from now on. You have to be purified. You have a Demon in you. That's why you've been behaving in the way you have done."

My eyeballs swivelled desperately as I attempted to look him in the eye.

"Jim," I said, "what are you planning on doing with me?"

In my heart of hearts I knew exactly what he was planning, but I couldn't bring myself to believe *it* was going to happen to *me*.

"I'm saving you, Brad," he said. "You have been evil, but deep down you're a good man, I can see that. It wasn't you who committed those sins, it was the Demons inside you. So I'm going to save you. I'm beginning by purifying you."

I had to know how it would end, even though it was obvious.

"What will you do when you've purified me?" I asked.

"When you've been purified for seven days, I will shave the top of your head. Then I will cut the shape of the holy cross of the Lord into the skin on the top of your head with a sharp knife. Next I will peel the skin back to reveal the skull beneath it, and I will tighten the vice until you feel pain. Then I will slowly tighten it some more until at least one of your eyeballs pops from its socket under the pressure.

You won't be dead at that point. You will still be very much alive, and able to feel the pain of the brace and bit that I will use to cut an opening in your skull from which the Demons may escape.

I will use a sharpened spatula to remove a significant portion of your brain tissue and evict the Demons from your soul. Finally, I will tighten the vice until your skull cracks under the pressure. When that happens you will probably die. But if you don't, you will die soon afterwards. At least, that's what most people do. Some of the more unfortunate ones cling on to life for a good while longer."

I reflected on those words.

I realised when Jim told me how it will all end that the only control I now have over my life during these, my final days, is what I dictate into this tape recorder.

So I decided to make the most of the time I had left by telling my own story, not his. And I myself have a legacy to leave. It is a legacy that will make the world sit up and take notice. One that will make me immortal.

I hope that one day Jim will publish this work, or that the tape will be found, and someone other than Jim will publish it, possibly as a book that will become a bestseller.

If you are one of the many fans who have been reading my columns in the Manchester Daily News, please excuse the quality of my prose. I have not had the opportunity to polish it up to my usual standard.

My heart aches for Sandra and for my two beloved children, Jack and Lucy. I will miss them forever.

I hope you have enjoyed my company, Dear Reader.

Jim has returned and is beginning to tighten up the vice. I can feel the sides of my skull being compressed closer together. The pressure, both psychological and physical, is too much to bear. It is time for me to say good-bye. It is indeed the end.

Sweet Lord, have mercy on my soul.

Good-bye.

THE END

LINER NOTES

At the age of sixteen I read *It Happened in Boston?* by Russell H Greenan, a novel I found remarkable (and still do).

My immediate first thought on finishing it was: I wish I'd written that.

Many years later I read *The Killer Inside Me* by Jim Thompson, another remarkable novel. Once more I thought: I wish I'd written that.

You can't write a book that's already been written, that would be an absurdity[1], so I parked those aspirations and got on with my life.

But one day I thought: those two novels, however different, share a single plot idea: they're both about an apparently rational person who goes off the rails and commits a series of murders.

This made me think that even though I couldn't write these favourites of mine, I could at least come up with a story that had something in common with them: the man who starts out normal and becomes a killer.

That was the genesis of Manchester Vice.

In order to ensure that it was as different as could

be from the books that'd inspired it, I added ingredients that weren't used by Greenan or Thompson.

Firstly, sibling rivalry.

Brad has this in bucket loads. His brother, Brian, is only ever seen through the distorting lens of Brad's eye. As a result, he can do nothing right.

Brad admits Brian has looked after himself and has the body of an athlete – but far from being worthy of praise, this makes him a "bastard".

While Brad is honest enough to describe his brother as "good-looking", he quickly adds "in a dated 50s movie-star kind of way."

He blames Brian for causing his father's heart attack. There is no evidence of this, and it is most unlikely that he did.

Even the fact that Brian has had short stories published isn't worthy of praise in Brad's view.

So intensely does he feel the rivalry with his brother that he persists with it well after his brother's death.

Second, the quest for eternal youth.

It is probably as old as our species, although it seems to have come to the fore in recent years.

Various characters pursue this goal in their own unique ways throughout the text. Brad's example is probably the one you'd be least advised to follow, however effective it proves for him.

There are some themes which, of course the novel has in common with its illustrious predecessors: love, death, and betrayal. I don't claim to have explored them in great depth, but they are certainly present.

Jenny the family cat is worth a mention: I introduced her because my work owes something to

Poe, and I wanted to make that clear. (Note: there is a cat in *It Happened in Boston* which doesn't fare too well; Greenan may have included his feline character for the same reason I did).

When, as a schoolboy, I studied *King Lear* in English Literature, my teacher told me that tragedy is about people who bring about their own downfall through fatal character flaws which compel them to make bad decisions.

Noir crime fiction is much like classical tragedy in that respect: the characters in noir crime make bad moral choices, and, once they have made them, they are doomed.

So it is with Brad Sharpe. He kills his brother, and after that, his fate is sealed – although there are any twists and turns as it plays out.

In closing, please don't for one moment think I put my work on a par with that of Russel H Greenan, Jim Thompson, or Edgar Allan Poe.

I don't.

But if you've enjoyed it, then I can live in hope that someday I might write something almost as good as those guys.

---

1. *As witness Pierre Menard, author of the Quixote* by Jorge Luis Borges

TO MY READERS:

Thank you for taking the trouble to read my novel. If you enjoyed it, please mention it to your friends and post a favourable review.

Feel free to let me know what you think of 'Manchester Vice' contact me on Facebook or Twitter: @jackstrange11
Your help is very much appreciated.

Many thanks.
Jack D McLean

Dear reader,

We hope you enjoyed reading *Manchester Vice*. Please take a moment to leave a review, even if it's a short one. Your opinion is important to us.

Discover more books by Jack D. McLean at

https://www.nextchapter.pub/authors/author-jack-mclean

Want to know when one of our books is free or discounted? Join the newsletter at

http://eepurl.com/bqqB3H

Best regards,

Jack D. McLean and the Next Chapter Team

ACKNOWLEDGMENTS

Thank you Akef Akbar, Director of Tyler Hoffman Solicitors in Wakefield & Halifax, for kindly advising on the police station scene in the novel. You helped me ensure that the scene is as authentic as possible.

Thank you Robert Bose and Axel Howerton for your sterling work on the first edition of this book.

Thank you Miika and the rest of the team at Next Chapter for doing such a great job of producing this edition of Manchester Vice and bringing it to the attention of readers.

Finally, thank-you to all the friends I have who've encouraged me with my writing. In no particular order, they are: Paul D, Denis, Paul D B, Pearl, Martin, Melinda, Paul M, Owen, Debbie, Marc, Julian, Sean, Phil, Cheshire Venom and Ted. (I hope I haven't left anybody out – if I have, I'm very sorry!).

Manchester Vice
ISBN: 978-4-86750-388-1
Mass Market

Published by
Next Chapter
1-60-20 Minami-Otsuka
170-0005 Toshima-Ku, Tokyo
+818035793528

4th June 2021

Lightning Source UK Ltd.
Milton Keynes UK
UKHW040642100822
407110UK00001B/93